Needled to Death

A Southern Quilting Mystery, Volume 15

Elizabeth Craig

Published by Elizabeth Spann Craig, 2021.

NEEDLED TO DEATH

First edition. October 26, 2021.

Written by Elizabeth Craig.

Chapter One

MEADOW DOWNEY CLEARED her throat after calling the meeting of the Village Quilters to order. Ordinarily, there would be some business addressed first—the minutes from the last meeting, updates on upcoming events, and that type of thing. But Meadow, when she was excited about something, had a very hard time containing herself, much less attend to the mundane aspects of a guild meeting.

And Meadow was, of course, anything but mundane. She stood there with her hair in a loose, long braid that hung to her waist, red glasses that she constantly pushed up on her nose, chunky white jewelry, and a typically-mismatched tunic and legging set. She beamed at the assembled quilters. "I'm so glad you're all here because I have something so thrilling to talk about. We're going to do another round-robin quilt! Remember how much fun we had the last time?"

Everyone beamed back except for Savannah Potter. Savannah was a quilter who worked with careful precision and had a loyal fondness for adherence to both her routine and geometric patterns. A willy-nilly quilt without very specific instructions was somewhat akin to a nightmare for her instead of a fun creative jaunt. Savannah's sister Georgia reached over and squeezed her hand, which made Savannah's worried frown relax a bit.

Meadow clapped her hands together and said, "I know, right? It was so much fun! Honestly, it's still one of my favorite quilts of all time. I realize Posy has it on display at the Patchwork Cottage, but I think she should have it on loan so we all get to spend some time with it. Wouldn't that be fun? It would be a quilt tour! Anyway, on to this next round-robin quilt. This time everything is going to work a little differently, ladies. I was speaking with some of the women from the Cut-Ups guild and we all thought a great way for us to get to know each other better was to have *joint* round-robin projects. Isn't that wonderful?"

There was a general murmur of cheerful approval from the room as Meadow grinned at them all.

"Because of the size of our groups, we'll make two quilts. So, like before, we're going to each do a square without knowing how the rest of the quilt looks. When we piece them together at the end, they're going to be a fabulous, unique bit of art."

"Or a different type of crazy quilt," muttered Savannah glumly, her heavy eyebrows pulling together.

Beatrice smiled sympathetically at her. But then, she was smiling at everyone right then because she had her grandbaby, Will, on her lap. From time to time, Will would reach up and studiously consider her face before reaching gingerly out for her nose or ear. Beatrice had learned not to put earrings in on the days she was going to be with Will. As much as she loved the little guy, pulling earrings was decidedly not behavior she wished to encourage.

Even better, Beatrice's daughter Piper was there with them today, even though it was a Friday afternoon. Piper had been working nearly full-time in the elementary school's office but her husband, Ash, recently received a raise and promotion at the college he worked for and she'd quickly cut back her hours to spend more time with Will.

Beatrice dragged her attention away from Will and back to Meadow who was answering questions about the round robin project, including the type of fabric they'd use and whether they should pre-wash it. They moved on to the size of the quilt next and got that established. And finally, at Savannah's urging, they did choose a loose color scheme of sorts so there would be some sort of coordination going on.

Guild member Posy, who owned the local quilting shop, said, "I did hear about a fun thing the Cut-Ups were doing with a round robin project of their own, some time ago."

Meadow put her hands on her hips. "Well, we *definitely* want to hear about that! We wouldn't want the Cut-Ups to have more fun than we do."

"I'm sure they don't," said Georgia quickly. "We have the best group of ladies. And men, of course, when Ash can join us."

Piper gave Beatrice a rueful look. Ash's raise and promotion seemed to directly coincide with a heavier teaching schedule and less time to pursue interests like quilting.

"Very true," said Posy, turning her gentle smile on Georgia. "We do have such nice people in our guild. What one of the Cut-Ups was telling me was that during their last round robin, they sent a little notebook around in the round robin box so each person could jot down some notes about their process or their thoughts during their round. It ends up being a journal for the project and is fun to revisit at the very end."

There was a murmur of approval around the room. They were meeting in Meadow's house this time—a converted barn with soaring skylit ceilings and quilts scattered everywhere. Boris, Meadow's huge dog of uncertain breeding, lifted his head to blearily check and see if scraps of food were on the floor before dropping off to snooze again. Usually, Boris was something of a menace during guild meetings—in his excitement nearly knocking guests down or sneakily managing to commandeer some of the food Meadow put out. But Meadow had discovered a trick, and now froze Kong chew toys stuffed full of oatmeal and plain yogurt for Boris to work on while the quilters came in. Apparently, working on the frozen Kong chews also served to make him very sleepy, which was another wonderful benefit.

After her big announcement, Meadow moved on to other guild business. Always a tremendous recruiter for the Village Quilters, she said, "I hope everyone has had the opportunity to welcome our guest today. Let me speak on behalf of everyone when I say a hearty *thank you* for coming over today. Jessica Brennan, everyone!"

Beatrice hid a smile. Meadow was calling out Jessica's name as if a rock star had made an appearance at the guild meeting. Jessica gave a small wave to everyone and an uncomfortable laugh. She was a young woman who seemed very eager about learning everything she could about quilting. She was tall with very straight, brown hair.

Meadow, who apparently didn't believe guild guests might be timid about speaking in front of veritable strangers, said, "Jessica, come on over and tell us a little about your quilts."

Jessica hesitated for a second before picking up the quilt she brought with her and joining Meadow at the front of the room. She cleared her throat and worked the quilt through her fingers for a few moments as she collected her thoughts.

Will, still on Beatrice's lap, shook his toy, which made a rattling noise that filled the silence. Everyone laughed and that made Jessica relax a little.

"So, I haven't been quilting as long as you all have. I'm really interested in learning the craft from a lot of different angles and I can't wait to hear what everyone is working on. I've spent some time with the Cut-Ups, too, because I'm trying to soak in as much information about the craft as possible," said Jessica. She spoke in a bit of a rush as if she was eager to sit back down again. "Right now, my focus has been on trying some experimental approaches with quilts." She gave everyone an apologetic look as if this might not go over too well, but the guild members all looked interested. Except Savannah, noted Beatrice, who couldn't be expected to be interested in anything other than her beloved geometrics.

Meadow asked, "And you're fairly new to town, aren't you? How do you like Dappled Hills?"

Jessica smiled, "It's a beautiful place and I love it here. I've been here almost a year now."

Meadow said with a mischievous look in her eyes, "And should we all suggest wonderful people for you to date?"

Beatrice gave a gusty sigh, which made Will turn and look at her soberly. She gave him a reassuring smile and cuddle. But Meadow was really the most incorrigible matchmaker.

Jessica chuckled. "I hope not. I think Carl would be a little concerned by that."

Meadow deflated a little. "Oh, you're married?"

"Three years," said Jessica with a grin.

Georgia piped up from her spot on Meadow's sofa. "Jessica is a teacher at Piper's and my school. I'm just excited that I was able to persuade her to come by."

Meadow still frowned in disappointment that her usual information sources had failed her this time by not telling her that Jessica was married. "That's very nice," she said absently in response to Georgia. "Jessica, can you show us the quilt you brought with you today?"

Jessica looked a little shy as she carefully held up the quilt. Beatrice perked up, leaning forward. It was quite good. The pattern looked like a winding maze of meandering cream-colored paths and the colors were shades of red. It was the kind of quilt that pulled you in and perhaps made you a bit dizzy as you looked at it.

Meadow beamed at Jessica. "That's marvelous, Jessica! Isn't it, everyone?"

There was enthusiastic applause from the group. Jessica gave them another quick smile and then hurried back to her seat with relief.

Jessica's quilt kicked off the whole "sew and tell" portion of the meeting and different members showed off what they'd been working on. Beatrice paid special attention when June Bug quietly held up her deceptively easy pinwheel quilt. She had overlaid netting to create a 3-D effect with the quilt and it had worked out beautifully. Beatrice decided it was time for her to try and do something a little more challenging of her own. She'd had a period of time where she'd gotten burned out and then reverted to easier projects but now felt she was ready to tackle something trickier. Currently, she was working on some colorful mini quilts to use for potholders, coasters, and quilted pillow cases. The projects were short and easy and were keeping her interested . . . for now. But she knew she was going to need something more complex soon.

Beatrice felt someone prod her in her side and saw that Miss Sissy, the elder stateswoman of the group, had pulled up a chair next to her. The old woman looked as madcap as ever, her wiry gray hair spilling out of her lopsided bun. She prompted Beatrice to hand over Will, her eyes demanding. It was fine with Will, who was fascinated by Miss Sissy's wild hair, bright button eyes, and cackling laugh. Miss Sissy had taken to making homemade toys for Will—usually noisemakers, which weren't going to be the best choice for a guild meeting.

Sure enough, the old woman handed Will a can of peanuts. Beatrice winced in anticipation since Miss Sissy ordinarily filled them with pennies. Luckily, she'd apparently filled them with seeds of some kind because they made more of a tinkling, swishing sound than the cacophony she'd expected. Will shook the can vigorously and smiled, his dimples appearing, as he listened to the seeds moving around.

Soon the meeting adjourned, although that was when most of the socializing took place. Jessica joined Beatrice and Miss

Sissy and reached tenderly out for Will who smiled fetchingly at her. Miss Sissy glowered in response at Jessica, sure that she had designs on the baby.

Jessica, fortunately, didn't seem to register the expression on Miss Sissy's face. Or, perhaps, she'd been warned that the fierce expression was a common one on the old woman's visage.

"Miss Sissy, Meadow was telling me that you've been quilting most of your life and that you came from generations of quilters," said Jessica.

Miss Sissy straightened a little in her chair but still looked suspiciously at Jessica as Will crowed and reached out for Jessica's nose.

Jessica chuckled and gave Will a hug. "I was wondering if I could see your quilts at some point. And if you might give me some pointers on quilting."

Miss Sissy considered this for a second before saying gruffly, "Don't know much about new stuff."

"I want to know about all different types of quilting," said Jessica. "I want to get better at quilting in every sense."

Miss Sissy thought for another couple of seconds before giving a brisk nod.

"Is there a time that might work for me coming over?" asked Jessica.

Beatrice hid a smile as Miss Sissy looked completely astounded at the idea that she dealt with time in slotted appointments instead of the vast wasteland of empty space that it was for her.

"Anytime is fine," she finally offered.

Jessica smiled at her. "I'll come over tomorrow around lunch. In fact, I'll bring lunch over. I'm going to make some spinach and tomato quiches later today and I'll bring them with me."

Miss Sissy now looked positively delighted at the prospect of Jessica's visit. Either Meadow had versed Jessica well on Miss Sissy's predilection for food or else Jessica had very good instincts. Either way, Miss Sissy was now totally won over.

However, Miss Sissy also saw trouble on the horizon in the form of Meadow. Meadow had that stubbornly-determined expression on her face that meant she intended to pluck up her grandson and spirit him away so that she could keep him all to herself. Miss Sissy quickly stood up and scuttled off, baby in tow, for the other side of the room.

Jessica blinked with surprise and Beatrice said, "Don't worry—it wasn't you. Miss Sissy saw Meadow coming and knew she wanted to take Will away from her."

Jessica smiled. "Got it. Well, that makes sense. At least Miss Sissy was willing to help me out and talk about her quilting. It'll be nice to visit with her tomorrow."

Beatrice frowned at Jessica's uncertain expression. "Have you run across quilters here who aren't willing to help out? I usually think of it as a pretty helpful community."

Jessica said reluctantly, "Well, maybe it's more that I've caught the person at the wrong time. I hate to speak poorly of someone, especially since I'm still so new in town."

Beatrice gave her a wry look. "Unfortunately, small towns are all about gossip. It's probably nothing I haven't heard before. Word spreads quickly here."

Jessica nodded. "It's just . . . well, do you know Flossie Powell?"

Chapter Two

AT THE MENTION OF FLOSSIE Powell, an image came up in Beatrice's mind of an elegant woman with a chignon wearing expensive clothes. "I know who she is and I've met her a few times, but I wouldn't say I really know her well. Isn't she supposed to be a speaker at one of our next meetings?" Beatrice tried to recall the business portion of the meeting she'd just attended. Will had been particularly fetching during that portion and Beatrice acknowledged she might have been distracted.

Jessica nodded. "That's what Meadow said. I know she has a lot of experience with quilting from all aspects and that she's been a quilt show judge on a high level. I've gone to a couple of Cut-Ups guild meetings and Flossie seemed like she was so knowledgeable from everything I heard her say. That's why I sought her out, like I've been trying to reach out to other people. Trying to find mentors." She hesitated and flushed a little. "That's not to say that I wouldn't be looking for advice from you, Beatrice. You've been doing this for a while, too, haven't you?"

Beatrice smiled at her. "No, not at all. My connection to quilting was from a very different angle. I was a curator at a museum that focused on Southern arts and crafts. I have a good deal of knowledge about the quilting craft, but not from personally doing it myself. It's been relatively recent that I started quilting. In a lot of ways, I feel like I'm still learning the ropes."

Jessica looked relieved that she hadn't inadvertently put her foot in her mouth. "Well, that's an important aspect of quilting, too. I'd love to talk with you about your experience at the museum one day. Anyway, I approached Flossie and she sort of rolled her eyes a little about meeting with me. I was pretty surprised because everyone that I've spoken with so far has been really welcoming and open about sharing what they know."

Beatrice nodded. "I'm sorry to hear that Flossie wasn't more open to meeting with you. Dappled Hills is a friendly town, generally."

"Exactly."

Beatrice said, "Maybe she was just busy right then? Did it seem like she didn't have time to fit anything in?"

"Well, it sounded like she did have an upcoming show she was working on with Dora Tucker. But I got the impression that it was more than just trying to fit me in. She didn't seem happy about the idea of being a mentor at all. But she did agree to meet with me tomorrow and take a look at my quilts to tell me her thoughts on them. After all, if she's judged events where there have been modern quilts, she'll know if I'm on the right track or not."

Beatrice gave her a thoughtful look. "Are you sure that's what you want? Do you need her validation for your work? That can be dangerous territory, especially for a new quilter."

Jessica said slowly, "I don't think I need her validation for my own self-satisfaction, but I think I need it to make sure I'm not wasting my time."

"I can tell you right now that you're not wasting your time," said Beatrice firmly. "You're on the right track. I was very impressed with the quilt you brought with you today and with your passion for the craft and the way you're trying to soak up all the information you can."

"Thank you," said Jessica, still looking a little uncertain. "I kind of lose the ability to tell if my quilting is any good or not. You know how it is—you get so wrapped up in the quilts that it's tough to have any sort of real perspective on them. I tend to think they look great but then when I see everyone else's quilts, they look so amazing that I'm sure I've got a long way to go."

Beatrice nodded. "I think most of us feel that way. Just try not to fall into the trap of comparing your work to other quilters' projects. You're doing something completely unique."

A little group of quilters came up to welcome Jessica then, so Beatrice walked away to get more of the food Meadow had set out. Meadow was quite a cook. Today, among fried green tomatoes, pimento cheese sandwich squares, Vidalia onion dip, and deviled eggs, she had mini tomato pies in ramekin bowls that looked absolutely amazing. Beatrice wanted to sample one before Miss Sissy ended up carting off most of the food. Beatrice was just taking one of them when she heard Piper chatting with Savannah behind her.

Piper grinned at her. "You and I must be on the same wavelength. I wanted to try the tomato pie, too."

Beatrice greeted Savannah and said, "Your Aunt Tiggy didn't make it today? How are things going with her?"

Aunt Tiggy, who'd raised Savannah and Georgia, had come for a long visit to Dappled Hills and had decided to stay put.

Savannah gave a dry laugh. "She had a conflict today, but I'm sure she'll be at the next meeting. She doesn't want to join the guild or really do much quilting, but she loves catching up with everyone. And things are going great now that she has her own apartment and isn't making dresses for Georgia and me anymore."

Beatrice smiled. The dresses had been matching ones and were pretty awful. Tiggy's heart was in the right place, but her style left much to be desired. When Tiggy had been staying with Savannah, she'd also been foisting very healthy food on her (that apparently wasn't seasoned at all). Junk food-loving Savannah had been pretty miserable. Fortunately, Tiggy had moved on to other interests, including dating a nice guy who was the local handyman. What was more, Tiggy had her own place now and wasn't staying with Savannah.

Piper, apparently on the same wavelength as her mother, asked lightly, "And she's not cooking for you anymore?"

Savannah gave a shudder. "No, thank goodness. I'm back to eating as unhealthily as I like."

Beatrice reflected that Savannah might be eating canned pasta, potato chips, and other junk food, but you certainly couldn't tell it to look at her angular figure.

Savannah cast a longing look over Meadow's spectacular spread of food and said, "Speaking of unhealthy eating, I should probably make myself a plate before Meadow starts clearing everything up."

She wandered away and Piper glanced around the large room. "I see Miss Sissy still has Will."

"Hanging on to him for dear life," said Beatrice wryly.

"That's because he's surrounded by his little fan club."

Sure enough, Miss Sissy was holding onto Will fiercely as he was surrounded by cooing guild members. Will, used to the spotlight, was grinning at all of them.

"I'm going to take advantage of this opportunity to eat in peace," said Piper. "Want to join me?"

Beatrice did. Although she loved just about every minute she could spend with her grandson, she did miss some of the one-on-one moments with her daughter since Will had been born. Beatrice served herself a ham biscuit and settled down on the sofa next to Piper to chat for a little while. Piper talked about Ash and how he was enjoying his promotion at the college and how much *she* was enjoying spending more time at home and with Will.

"I'm trying to keep him busy, though, since he enjoys being out and about and seeing people. We're going to go to the next library story time for toddlers. He had so much fun at the last one that I think we'll try to make all of them. Would you and Meadow like to go?"

Beatrice smiled. "I'm sure Meadow going is a foregone conclusion. You know how much she loves doing as much with Will as possible. And I do, too—you can count me in. How could I possibly turn down seeing Will and being at the library at the same time? The library is one of my favorite places."

"I'll email you the information on it. I can't remember off the top of my head which day it is."

Beatrice snorted. "There's nothing going on in my schedule that can't be adjusted to make story time, believe me."

"That's not completely true," said Meadow who'd just swooped over from a conversation with Jessica. "Tomorrow evening, right before supper, we're going to go over to Flossie's house and pick up round-robin materials from the Cut-Ups."

"Yes, but that's surely not time-specific. Flossie can't be that much of a taskmaster."

Meadow said, "You clearly don't know Flossie very well. She *is* that much of a taskmaster and she wanted us there at a specific time because she's having people over for dinner or something."

Piper said quickly, "That doesn't matter because I'm certain the library story time isn't going to happen in the evening. Evenings are not a wonderful time for toddlers. Or their moms."

Beatrice chuckled. "I remember. I called that fussy time of the day 'happy hour' when you were that age. A glass of wine made it go a lot better."

Meadow said loyally, "Not that Will is ever really fussy."

Piper and Beatrice shared a smile. Will would always be perfect in Meadow's eyes. "He's a very good boy," agreed Piper.

Beatrice said, "Going back to Flossie, Meadow, I'm not totally sure I understand why it's necessary for both of us to go over and get the materials from her. Surely that's more of a one-person job. Or she could simply leave the fabric in a bag on her front porch for someone to pick up."

"It was my idea for us to go over there. I thought it would be good for both of us to get to know Flossie a little better. And sort of a good will gesture between the Village Quilters and the Cut-Ups. That's also the reason why I was getting Flossie over to give a talk to the group next time."

"You're not trying to spirit her away from the Cut-Ups, are you?" asked Beatrice.

Piper hid a smile. Meadow's recruitment activities were tough to curtail. She was always very enthusiastic about obtaining new members for the guild.

"Of course not," said Meadow with dignity, although her cheeks were a little flushed. "That would be stealing, wouldn't it? I just think that she has so much experience and a lot she could teach our group. She was a judge on the big quilt show circuits, is NACQJ certified. That's the National Association of Certified Quilt Judges, in case you didn't know. I know she can give us so many tips on improvement. Of course, if she succumbs to our welcoming environment here and decides to defect, that would be good, too."

Beatrice said in a low voice, "Are we sure she's eager to do that?"

"To defect? Oh, I don't know," said Meadow. She looked decidedly intrigued by the possibility.

"No, I mean, is she eager to give tips to help us improve? Jessica was telling me a few minutes ago that Flossie didn't seem very enthusiastic about giving her quilting advice or evaluating her quilts."

Meadow knit her brows together, suddenly making herself look quite ferocious. "Really? Why on earth would she behave that way toward a young quilter when we're trying to draw more young people into the craft?"

Beatrice held up her hands as if to ward off Meadow's fury. "I come in peace, Meadow. Look, it was just Jessica's impression. She might have been a little sensitive. Or maybe Flossie just came off as disinterested but there's something else going on in the background. She could have a lot going on in her personal life right now."

But Meadow couldn't be pacified. "That's simply ridiculous. Was Flossie somehow feeling threatened by Jessica's talent? Because she *is* very talented, don't y'all agree?"

Beatrice and Piper nodded. Beatrice said, "I was impressed with the quilt she brought in today and would love to see more of her different projects."

"Exactly. Which is a normal response. That Flossie! I have a mind to have a word with her when we see her tomorrow evening," huffed Meadow.

Beatrice said mildly, "I thought it was supposed to be some sort of good will mission. At any rate, Flossie did apparently agree to meet with Jessica, even if she wasn't overly enthusiastic about it. They're supposed to see each other tomorrow at some point."

This mollified Meadow a little. She said with a sniff, "Well, at least she came to her senses. I hope that goes well."

Beatrice added, "And Miss Sissy agreed to show Jessica her quilts tomorrow at lunch."

This made Meadow smile. "Good old Miss Sissy. Just when you think she's absolutely insufferable, she goes and does something sweet."

Piper carefully changed the subject to Meadow's grandson and Meadow happily made the leap. They talked about Will's latest playdate with a new friend from preschool and how it was mostly spent in parallel play with the friend.

After a few minutes of chatting and nibbling, everyone started meandering out and thanking Meadow for hosting. Boris grinned at them all as they left and looked proud as everyone told him what a good dog he'd been. He gave them a lazy grin while still nosing the Kong to see if any yogurt remained in the bottom of the chew toy.

Piper glanced at her watch as she stood by her car. "I feel like I need to do something to keep Will awake for a while. He's looking really sleepy after all the activity at Meadow's, but if he falls asleep now, he'll be all messed up tonight."

"Do you have your stroller with you?"

Piper nodded. "I keep an umbrella stroller in the trunk now, just in case."

"Why don't you drive next door to my place and park?" suggested Beatrice. "Then we can take Will on a stroller ride downtown. He's always so alert when we go on rides. It should keep him awake for a while."

Piper thought that was a great idea. Minutes later, they set out for downtown Dappled Hills. Beatrice quickly went inside to collect Noo-noo, feeling that her corgi could also stand to stretch her short legs.

Posy passed them in her car a few minutes later on her way back home. "What a darling little parade!" she said, smiling at them and then waving as she drove off down the road.

It was actually fairly busy downtown, giving Will lots of things to look at. There was a mother coming out of a store clutching a bunch of brightly-colored balloons, some of which had cartoon characters and stars on them. Will was mesmerized and she stopped to let him gingerly reach out and touch some of them.

There was a large man walking a very small dog. Noo-noo and the dog said hi to each other while Will watched with interest.

And then there was the sound of an animated discussion of some kind going on down one of the side streets. After a moment, the discussion sounded heated. Then it accelerated into argument territory.

Piper and Beatrice hadn't yet reached the street where this loud disagreement was taking place, but Beatrice thought she recognized one of the voices. "Doesn't that sound like Dora Tucker?"

Piper raised her eyebrows. "It does, now that you mention it. I sure wouldn't want to get on her bad side."

Beatrice tended to agree. "Dora has a lot of qualities I admire. But I definitely wouldn't want to engage in an argument with her."

Sure enough, when they reached the corner, they saw Dora in a standoff with none other than Flossie Powell. Dora had her hands on her hips and Flossie had her arms crossed in front of her. Both of them had belligerent expressions on their faces.

Chapter Three

"I DON'T KNOW WHY I even try to talk to you," said Flossie in a cold voice. "You never listen. You just do whatever you want to do."

Flossie seemed exceedingly put-out. Beatrice didn't know Flossie well, but ordinarily when she came across her, she had a big smile on her face. She seemed to have a very outgoing personality, which had likely served her well for all those years on the quilt show circuit. She was an elegant woman with brown eyes and gray hair that was pulled back at the nape of her neck in a chignon. Now she looked very stern and her expression was icy.

Dora, on the other hand, looked like she was in the process of exploding. Her frizzy hair was fairly bristling with indignation. "I *do* listen," she said in response to Flossie. "Everyone can tell you that."

Beatrice gave Piper a small smile as they slowly kept walking. Dora might listen. But she always did whatever she thought was best. Dora was excellent at organizing and felt she should rely on the one person who'd never let her down—herself.

They'd passed the side street now, but Flossie's voice followed them. "If they tell me that, it's because they're lying, Dora. Great leaders must learn to listen and to delegate. I have grave concerns about the way you're organizing that quilt show."

Piper said under her breath, "Oh my gosh. I can't imagine saying something like that to Dora. Dora's organized *everything* perfectly for years. At the church, for the guilds. Fairs, dances, fundraisers. It all runs like clockwork."

"I know. But I guess Flossie has been involved in bigger shows and probably for a longer period of time than Dora has." Beatrice shook her head. "Still, this is yet another strike against Flossie today."

Piper said, "I guess they're talking about the regional show that's going to be in Lenoir?"

"They must be. Well, hopefully they'll work it out."

They walked down to the park and down the shady paths so Will could see all the older children running around on the playground. He watched with big, intent eyes.

"How about if we put him in the baby swing?" asked Beatrice. "Then he can feel like he's participating and still watch the big kids playing."

A minute later, Will was happily swinging through the air, his wispy hair swooshing back and forth as he went. He smiled as he saw the big kids climbing on a man-made rock wall, sliding down plastic slides (and sometimes walking up them the wrong way, causing their mothers to fuss), and building castles in the sandbox. Noo-noo grinned at Will as he sailed back and forth, apparently thinking it was funny to see the little guy sailing through the air.

"How are things going?" asked Beatrice as she watched Will's happy face.

Piper gave her a cheery smile. "Oh, it's all great. Will is learning more and more every day. I've had such a good time sitting down with him and reading—I swear he follows along and sometimes I see him mouthing the words as we go."

Beatrice gave her a gentle look. "But that's how *Will* is doing. I asked how *you* were doing."

Piper took a deep breath. "I don't know that I've really even thought that much about it. You know how young moms are—we just don't have the time to stop and contemplate." She paused and considered the question carefully. "I guess I feel sort of guilty."

"Guilty?"

"Yes. That might seem sort of weird, but it's how I feel when I think about it. I feel guilty that I'm not spending 100% of my time with Will because I'm working. But then I also feel guilty about cutting back on my hours at work and putting stress on Ash to earn a living for all of us. Basically, I feel guilty no matter what."

Beatrice said, "I think that's a mother's lot in life."

"Did you feel the same way?"

Beatrice snorted. "All the time. You know I was working a lot at the art gallery when you were little. Luckily, your father had a flexible enough job that he could cover for me whenever I got stuck at work. Then, when your father died, I felt especially bad about all the hours I was putting in as a curator."

Piper reached over and gave her mother a hug. "I get it, but you had to get food on the table. And I was a teenager at the time—it's not like I was a little kid."

"You still needed your mom, though, especially after you lost your dad." Beatrice, thinking back, still remembered that pull—that feeling that she wasn't doing the right thing, no matter what she was doing.

"Well, you absolutely did the best you could. And I ended up turning out all right," said Piper with a grin.

"I'll say. And Will is going to end up just fine, too. You're doing a fabulous job raising him, and so is Ash. When you're working, Will is hanging out with his grandmothers and a motley assortment of hangers-on," added Beatrice with a laugh, thinking of Miss Sissy.

"Thanks, Mama. You've made me feel better."

"I'm always here anytime you need to talk," said Beatrice.

They chatted for a few more minutes on lighter topics and then Piper said, "I think it's safe to take him back home now. I should probably start making some supper and Will's got to be hungry soon, too."

They strolled leisurely back, seeing a cat, two dogs on leashes, and a bright-eyed robin on the way back to Beatrice's house, which they pointed out to the baby.

"I'll let you know when the story time at the library is," said Piper as she strapped Will into his car seat. "Thanks for taking the walk with me."

Beatrice hugged Piper and then Will as Noo-noo grinned at them. Then she headed into the house to feed the little corgi.

After feeding Noo-noo, she realized that perhaps she should consider what the humans in the house should have for supper. It was still hard to really think about eating again after the filling, delicious food she'd had at Meadow's house. She was staring blankly at the contents of the fridge and feeling decidedly uninspired when her husband, Wyatt, came through the door.

Beatrice shut the fridge door to walk over and give him a kiss. The kiss was a little more fervent than she'd originally intended because Wyatt was holding a tote bag filled with delicious-smelling food.

He gave her a tight hug after the kiss and grinned at her. "Are you that happy to see me, or does it have more to do with the fact that I'm bringing supper in with me?"

"Both! I was just staring at the contents of our refrigerator and wondering if I figure out something to cook with eggs and tuna salad. Fortunately, we don't have to be guinea pigs for that experiment."

Wyatt said, "Well, I wish I could take all the credit for bringing in supper, but the truth of the matter is that Darla Kitchens brought it in for us at the church office a few minutes ago. Edgenora has some, too."

"I'll be sure to write Darla a note. That was sweet of her. And it makes me especially excited to eat supper, knowing that she was the one who cooked it. She's an amazing cook."

Although Beatrice wasn't at all sure she was hungry after all she'd eaten at the guild meeting, she found her appetite quickly returned to her as soon as she heated up the food and put it on plates. Darla had made lemon pepper chicken with quinoa and it looked absolutely delectable. Green beans were on the side along with some of Darla's fluffy, buttery biscuits.

"How was your day today?" asked Wyatt as they made quick work of the food on their plates.

"It was good. The guild meeting was fun and I got to catch up with everyone there. Piper was there with Will, too, so I had lots of cuddle time with the baby."

Wyatt said, "And Meadow hosted it, right? How was Boris?"

It was a good question, considering how many times Meadow's dog had either had to be exiled to a bedroom or had been highly disruptive during guild meetings. "Actually, he was surprisingly laid-back. Meadow had made Kongs for him and frozen them and he was absorbed with trying to lick the yogurt and oatmeal out of them. I think he's starting to relax a little more as he's getting older. The meeting itself went well, too." She told him about the round robin quilt. "Apparently, Meadow and I will be going around to Flossie Powell's house tomorrow evening to pick up some materials for the quilts."

"Flossie is with the Cut-Ups guild?"

"That's right," said Beatrice. She frowned. "There was actually some drama around her today, too. We had a visitor today at the meeting—Jessica Brennan. She's a younger woman who's really excited about learning everything she can about quilting. Jessica said she was visiting both guilds and just sort of soaking up information. Anyway, she was telling me that Flossie hadn't exactly been warm and welcoming to her when Jessica asked if Flossie could evaluate her quilt."

Wyatt raised his eyebrows. "And Flossie is something of an expert, I'm gathering?"

"She's been a quilt show circuit judge, which makes her very much of an expert in these parts. Jessica just looked so deflated when she was talking about Flossie that it put my back up a little. The quilting community here has always been really supportive and encouraging of other quilters."

Wyatt asked, "Did Jessica bring a quilt to the meeting?"

"She did. And I think she has a lot of natural talent. Her interest seems to be mostly modern quilts and experimental methods. I did tell Jessica I thought she had talent and she perked up a little when I told her that. And then, funny thing—Piper and I were taking Will on a stroller ride downtown and spotted Flossie in an argument with Dora Tucker."

"It sounds like Flossie might be having a bad week," said Wyatt ruefully.

Beatrice smiled indulgently at him. "Or she's like that all the time. The jury's out. You're nice to give her a pass, Wyatt."

"I don't think I know Flossie," said Wyatt thoughtfully. "Is she new to town?"

"Relatively so, I believe. I remember Posy mentioning her a year or so ago when Flossie went to the Patchwork Cottage to get supplies. Posy told me at the time that Flossie had moved here to be closer to her sister."

"Oh, who's her sister?" Wyatt took a sip of his iced tea.

"Alice Hall. I know her from the library and I think I've seen her at church a few times, too."

Wyatt nodded. "She's a member. I'm sure it must be nice for Alice to have family living nearby now."

Beatrice smiled again. She wasn't at all convinced that Alice was excited to have Flossie live in Dappled Hills, especially if Flossie was as difficult as she seemed. But it was nice that Wyatt thought so.

They finished up eating and then cleared the table together. Wyatt put the remaining food away and Beatrice put the dishes in the dishwasher. Noo-noo watched them from a distance, ever-hopeful that one of them might be extremely clumsy and drop food on the floor. To her disappointment, they both did their respective tasks with utmost coordination.

"What should we do tonight?" asked Wyatt. "Television? Listen to music? Go for a walk?"

Beatrice chuckled. "Well, the smart thing for us to do after a meal like that is to take a walk to help it digest. I know I ate too much, anyway. And that doesn't even count everything I consumed at Meadow's house."

Wyatt looked guilty for a moment. "I have a confession to make."

Beatrice grinned at his expression. "That sounds ominous, Wyatt. What sort of misdeed could you possibly have done?"

"Oh, I do plenty of them. But today, I neglected to tell you what I had for lunch today."

Beatrice raised her eyebrows. "I thought you just had the lunch I sent along with you today. A turkey sandwich, blueberries, and a granola bar."

Wyatt patted his stomach ruefully. "No, that's going to be my lunch tomorrow, I'm afraid. I've left it in the fridge at the church. I had an unexpectedly large lunch and now I think I'm going to be eating a bunch of salads in the next few days. Eugenia Wainwright came by the church today with fried chicken, mashed potatoes, biscuits, cornbread, and corn on the cob."

"Sounds like a carbohydrate extravaganza," said Beatrice dryly. "What possessed her?"

"Well, she did it out of the goodness of her heart, of course. She wanted to show her appreciation for the church staff."

Beatrice said, "Oh, that's right. She'd had that broken hip and we all brought food for weeks."

"Exactly. Anyway, we've had a couple of very generous members of the congregation bring food to the church today."

"I'll say!" Beatrice paused. "It sounds like we really *should* be taking that walk. But the fact of the matter is that I'm pretty tired and I just don't think I can rise to the occasion. You could take a walk by yourself, though. Or with Noo-noo."

The corgi pricked her ears upon hearing her name. She looked just about as sleepy as they did, though.

Wyatt said, "I think I'm pretty worn out, myself, actually. Maybe we can table the walk until tomorrow. Want to listen to music and read instead?"

It was a much better plan to Beatrice's way of thinking. They whiled away the next few hours with books, jazz music, and a sleeping corgi at their feet.

THE NEXT DAY WAS A quieter one for Beatrice. She got some housework done that she'd been putting off—the plastic containers in her kitchen cabinet had gotten out of control so she weeded a number of those out and organized and stacked the remaining ones. Inspired by her success with organizing, she then weeded out some of her clothes to take to Goodwill. There were a few tops that she kept thinking she was going to wear but never did. She knew now that she always seemed to wear the same seven outfits, no matter how many things she had in her closet. Beatrice also reminded herself not to buy more brightly-colored outfits. She liked the *idea* of wearing bright colors, but never chose them when it was time to get dressed.

Beatrice then took Noo-noo on a long walk to make up for the walk she and Wyatt didn't have after supper last night. This time she chose to stroll around the small lake across town, as a change of pace. Then she looked at her watch and realized she should hurry back home before Meadow picked her up for their errand to pick up the round robin supplies from Flossie.

Sure enough, Meadow was right on time and gave a jaunty toot of her van's horn to let Beatrice know she'd arrived. This made Noo-noo bark excitedly at the door so Beatrice tossed her a couple of treats as she walked out.

"Hi there," said Meadow cheerily as Beatrice climbed into the van. "How has your day been?"

"Quiet but productive," said Beatrice with satisfaction. "And I can't ask for better than that. What's yours been like?"

"A bit more hectic," admitted Meadow. "I realized paying the power bill had somehow slipped by me so I had to run over to the electric company and pay it in person. Then I realized there were a whole *slew* of bills that I'd forgotten about and so I ended up driving all over town with my checkbook in hand."

Beatrice raised her eyebrows. "That doesn't sound like you, Meadow."

"I know, but I remember what put me in this position to begin with and it had to do with Flossie."

"Flossie seems to be causing all sorts of issues lately," said Beatrice dryly. "What did she do this time?"

"It was a few weeks ago and she decided to visit me in person about the round robin and the regional quilt show. She texted me just a few minutes before she showed up. I usually don't care about what the state of my house looks like, but it's *Flossie*."

Beatrice nodded. Meadow's house was always a little chaotic but it wasn't ever truly messy—it was just cluttered. With Flossie's aura of elegance, refinement, and perfection, Beatrice could imagine her turning up her nose at clutter and especially at chaos.

Meadow sighed. "Anyway, I ran around the house, picking papers up and throwing them haphazardly into the coat closet. Then I had to do something about Boris. I knew Flossie would be wearing some sort of expensive designer outfit and Boris would jump on her and get mud on her clothes."

"He was *so* good during the guild meeting," said Beatrice. "I don't think I've ever seen him that calm."

Meadow beamed at her. "He was, wasn't he? The Kong really helped. Plus, I think it was also because Will was there and he was just quietly making sure the baby was okay. Will seems to have a calming effect on Boris. But Will *wasn't* there when Flossie visited, so I put Boris out in the yard for a little while with some treats."

"I'm guessing when Flossie left, you forgot to pull the papers and things from the closet? And some of the papers were the bills?"

Meadow nodded sadly. "That's right. It was lucky that I remembered today. Ramsay made some sort of comment about how tidy the house was and I snapped my fingers and realized the bills were still in the closet and *that's* why everything was so neat. And that's when my day spiraled out of control."

"That would be easy to have happen. That's why I have all of our bills on autopay and have asked for paperless billing."

Meadow sighed. "I've thought about doing that and then I forget as soon as I have the thought. You know what I really need? A good bout of spring cleaning. I need to give that old barn a real good going-over."

"What kinds of things do you usually tackle when you spring clean? Maybe you can inspire me. I keep on top of the everyday cleaning, but sometimes I feel like I don't see some of the stuff that builds up over time."

Meadow said, "Well, once I really get cracking, I clean my oven, defrost my freezer, wipe my baseboards, wipe down my window sills, clean the dryer vent—you know, that kind of stuff."

"I suddenly feel the urge to assess what the cottage needs to have done," said Beatrice wryly. "I think it might have been a while since I thought about those different areas."

"I know—we stay busy, especially with watching little Will. Anyway, I'll feel so much better once I get everything in order. Plus, I need to sit down and have a serious admin day where I get paperless billing set up, like you were talking about."

"Once it's set up, then you don't have to worry about it anymore. It's just that the set-up is sort of a pain." Beatrice started paying attention to her surroundings outside of the car. "Gosh, where exactly are we going? I feel as if we're heading out of town."

"We're driving to a very fancy area right on the side of a mountain," said Meadow. "I'm thinking Flossie must have quite the gorgeous view from her back windows."

"It sounds like an expensive place. Do you know what Flossie did for a living? I mean, besides being a quilt show judge."

"Well, quilting is her passion, as she always says, but she was in banking before that. Something to do with information technology if you can believe that. She was apparently a major executive at one of the big banks in Charlotte." Meadow stuck her tongue out between her teeth in concentration as she navigated around the twisty bends of the mountain road.

"I'm not surprised she climbed the ranks like that. She seems like the sort of person who does everything well."

"Oh, she *is*. It's fairly irritating, actually. You know how I enjoy cooking and I fancy myself a pretty good low-key cook?"

Beatrice nodded. "I'd say you're much better than 'pretty good.' At least in terms of homestyle cooking."

Meadow smiled again as she slowed down around a particularly treacherous curve. "That's very sweet of you! Anyway, I'd never presume to have Flossie over for dinner or take her a meal because it would seem far too pedestrian for her."

"Ah. She's *that* kind of cook."

"That's right," said Meadow. "She's an epicurean. But not just that—she's also something of a gourmet cook. I've heard that she makes spectacular meals . . . the type of recipes that take all day long and have very particular ingredients."

Beatrice frowned. "I wonder where someone actually procures those very particular ingredients in Dappled Hills?"

Meadow shrugged a shoulder. "Who knows? There's not a lot of that kind of fancy cooking going on around here. Perhaps she drives to another town. Or maybe she orders the ingredients for her creations online. At any rate, invitations to her dinners are supposed to be coveted." The GPS told her she was approaching her destination. "Ah, here we go."

But when Meadow and Beatrice pulled up to the house, there were several police cars and an ambulance in front.

Chapter Four

"HEAVENS! WHAT ON EARTH is going on?" demanded Meadow.

Beatrice had found that Meadow could be very protective over quilters, in general. She didn't like to think of any of them in trouble in any way. And, from what she could tell, Flossie certainly seemed to be in some kind of trouble.

"I'm not sure," said Beatrice cautiously. She peered out the passenger window. "Isn't that Flossie's sister there? Alice Hall?"

Meadow gasped. "It certainly is. But why isn't Alice inside with her sister? If Flossie is having some sort of medical emergency, shouldn't she be next to her? If she's in that ambulance, shouldn't Alice be holding her hand?"

Beatrice continued looking out the window. Then she said slowly, "The police seem busy, but they're not running. You'd think, if it was a medical emergency, that the police would be trying to help the EMTs get Flossie to the hospital as quickly as possible."

"We should ask Alice what's going on," said Meadow with determination.

But Alice was already moving away, also with determination. Her back was straight and she pushed her pair of black glasses up her nose. Beatrice could tell that she'd spotted them but had decided to keep moving. She got into her car and quickly drove away.

Meadow frowned. "She's left," she said, unnecessarily.

"Meadow, I have the feeling that something is very wrong with Flossie."

"Then why isn't her sister staying with her?" persisted Meadow.

"I'm wondering if Flossie might not be dead," said Beatrice carefully.

Although this possibility must surely have occurred to Meadow, she'd obviously buried it, not wanting to think that something like that could have happened to her fellow quilter. She drooped a bit and nodded. Then she said, eyes narrowed, "We're going to speak with Ramsay."

"He's looking pretty busy right now," said Beatrice slowly.

Meadow's husband, the Dappled Hills police chief, was indeed looking busy. He was speaking with other police officers that Beatrice suspected were from the state police. He must have felt their eyes on him because he glanced to the side and spotted them. He appeared to grimace when he saw Meadow's face. Meadow opened the van's door to hop out and Ramsay quickly held up a finger to ask for a moment.

As soon as he finished speaking with the other officers, he strode over, a serious expression on his face. He was a short, balding man with kind eyes. Right now, he looked just as determined as Meadow did.

"Hi there," he said cautiously, "What are you two doing here?"

Meadow knit her brows ferociously. "We're here on quilting business. What's happening with Flossie?"

Ramsay decided to sidestep her question by asking a question of his own. "Did Flossie know you were coming?"

Beatrice nodded and Meadow exclaimed, "Of course she did! We're not in the habit of knocking on people's doors right before suppertime without an invitation."

Ramsay took his little notebook out of his shirt pocket and jotted down a note. He sighed and said, "I'm afraid something has happened to Flossie."

"We saw the ambulance and the police cars, Ramsay, so that's not a surprise. What's going on?" Meadow was getting more and more agitated, despite Ramsay's gentle approach.

"She's passed away," he said carefully. "Someone dialed 911 from her house and when we arrived, we discovered her dead. I'm sorry, Meadow. Were you two friends?"

Meadow sat back in her seat, looking deflated. "Sort of. We had a joint project together—the Cut-Ups and the Village Quilters. Oh, this is terrible."

Beatrice cleared her throat, looking again at the state police, now going in wearing hooded coveralls. "I take it this isn't a natural death?"

"I'm afraid not," said Ramsay in a regretful tone. "Although we're establishing all the details now."

"Is Alice all right?" Beatrice asked. "We saw her leave a few minutes ago."

Ramsay shook his head and held his hands out. "She seemed like she might be in shock to me, but she refused medical care. And Alice Hall isn't the kind of person you can force to do anything she doesn't want to do."

Beatrice nodded.

Meadow, sensing a mission, straightened back up in her seat. "Beatrice, we should go visit Alice and make sure she's okay. And bring her some food."

Ramsay briefly closed his eyes.

Beatrice said cautiously, "Maybe we should let her be for tonight. We could head over there tomorrow morning with a breakfast casserole. You make wonderful breakfast casseroles."

Meadow shook her head, looking resolved. "If she's in shock, then someone should check on her. No one else knows about this right now—we're in a very quiet area of town. You and I should be the ones to do it."

Ramsay said, "I need to go. Meadow, try to be discreet if you do go to Alice's house. And don't pry."

Meadow blinked in surprise. "I'm *never* nosy. Only concerned."

Ramsay hurried off and Meadow started up the van again. "Let's see. Time is of the essence, so we should pick up food instead of making it ourselves."

Beatrice said, "Let's run by June Bug's bakery. I seem to remember that Alice is a vegetarian. Not a vegan, though, so she should be fine with eggs and cheese. June Bug has expanded into quiches and I know she has some vegetable ones. Besides, something light might hit the spot."

"You're right. Alice wouldn't want a heavy meal at a time like this—she probably doesn't have any appetite at all. An excellent idea, Beatrice!"

June Bug's bakery was very busy and it took a few minutes for Meadow and Beatrice to get to the front of the line. It also took some customers quite a while to pick what they wanted to eat. But Beatrice could forgive them that. When faced with a tempting case of pastries, cakes, doughnuts, and other delights, it would be tough to make up your mind. Her niece, Katy, gave them a shy wave from a table in the shop where she was doing homework with a friend.

June Bug gave them a pleased smile when they finally got to the front of the line. Beatrice said, "It's so busy here! You must be totally exhausted."

But June Bug's smile widened. "Makes the day go much quicker."

Besides, Beatrice reflected, June Bug had always displayed enormous amounts of energy and a tremendous work ethic.

Even Meadow seemed to realize this wasn't the time to talk with a long line behind them. They quickly picked up a broccoli and cheese quiche and a fruit cup that June Bug had in the display case and headed on their way.

Alice lived in a modest house in an older section of Dappled Hills. Her front walkway was carefully swept and her yard was very tidy with perfectly-pruned bushes lining the outside of the brick house.

Meadow tapped lightly on the door and a minute later a cautious-looking Alice peered out the window to the side of the door. Meadow smiled at her and Alice hesitated before slowly opening the door.

Alice's face was drawn and she looked completely worn out. Beatrice quickly said, "Alice, we're so sorry about your sister. We found out because we'd arranged to meet with Flossie and pick up some quilting materials."

Meadow piped up, "We saw you there, too, and wanted to check up on you. We know it must have been such a terrible shock."

Alice seemed to hesitate again, trying to decide whether she wanted to invite Meadow and Beatrice in or not. Then she held the door open and said politely, "Please, won't you come in?"

Meadow bounded in and Beatrice followed at a bit more sedate pace. Alice said, "Thanks so much to you for the food. I love quiche."

"I'll put it in the fridge for you," said Meadow, heading off in what appeared to be the direction of the kitchen as Alice directed Beatrice to sit on an old but comfy-looking sofa in the small, book-lined living room.

Meadow came back quickly—despite denying being nosy, she didn't want to miss anything.

Alice sat down in a threadbare armchair and gave them a stressed smile. "I'm sorry I didn't stop to speak when I saw you two at Flossie's. I did see you there, but I really felt at a loss for words. I still sort of feel that way now."

Meadow made an expansive dismissive gesture that very nearly knocked over some knick-knacks on the small table next to her. "It wasn't the time to worry about social niceties. You'd just had some terrible news."

Alice nodded, absently rubbing her hand against the side of her head. "It was terrible news, for sure."

Beatrice was just marveling at Alice's composure when a single tear slid down her cheek. She impatiently slid it away with her finger. "Sorry," she said crisply.

Meadow said, "Oh goodness, Alice! Don't apologize to us. You must be devastated."

Alice considered this carefully and then shook her head. "Not exactly devastated. I think what I'm feeling is guilt. I'm sixty-seven years old. Flossie was my little sister. If she was in any danger at all, I feel I should have known about it and protected her from it."

Beatrice and Meadow shared a glance. It was as Ramsay had said—not a natural death.

"What happened? I mean ... if you feel like you can talk about it," said Meadow quickly.

Alice absently rubbed at her forehead. "I was here at home and doing some weeding in the yard. I heard a car drive up and saw Ramsay's police cruiser." She looked at Meadow. "I appreciated him coming here himself and not calling me on the phone." She looked down at her hands again. "When Ramsay told me that Flossie had passed, I immediately asked him if she'd had a heart attack."

Beatrice asked, "Did she have cardiac problems?"

Alice shook her head. "Not as far as I'm aware. But I'd always warned Flossie that she got too worked up about things beyond her control. She had something of a temper and her face would get red when she was upset, which always seemed like a high blood pressure issue to me. Flossie did like to be in control."

Beatrice thought back to Flossie's argument with Dora Tucker the day before in downtown Dappled Hills. Dora was also someone who liked to be in charge.

Alice continued, "Poor Flossie was always so Type-A. She didn't like it when her day got off-schedule or if her routine was messed up in any way."

Meadow said, "That's why Beatrice and I were at her house right on time. We knew Flossie appreciated punctuality."

Alice sighed. "When Ramsay told me, I had such a hard time believing Flossie could be dead that I drove over there myself. You're right about Flossie appreciating punctuality and it was sweet of you to think of that before going over there. I'm afraid it would have been a very short visit with you even if Flossie *had* been alive. She was in the middle of preparing a gourmet dinner when she was murdered and the timing was everything when she cooked." She put her hand over her mouth. "Sorry. Ramsay asked me not to share that particular detail. Could you keep it under your hat?"

Meadow, Beatrice reflected, was already well-aware of Flossie's gourmet cooking proclivity. But the fact that she was cooking a fancy meal when she died was new information.

"Of course we can," said Meadow. She shook her head. "That Ramsay. He doesn't like any sort of information to circulate at all."

"The only reason I know that is because I'd called her when she was cooking and she was quite curt with me. Anyway, I'm sure she'd have greeted you both at the door, handed over the supplies you needed, and then gone right back to what she was doing. I wasn't at all surprised that she was concocting a fancy meal when she died." She shook her head. "I mostly eat microwave meals, but not Flossie. The quiche will be such a treat tonight—thanks."

Beatrice said in a gentle voice, "You shouldn't feel guilty about what happened. If you *had* been there to protect her, you might have been a victim, yourself. I know Flossie cared about you and wouldn't have wanted anything to happen to you. After all, she moved here to be closer to you."

Alice gave a strangled laugh. "I feel terrible saying this, but I firmly believe Flossie moved to Dappled Hills to sort of show me up." She rubbed her head again. "Again, I feel so guilty saying these kinds of things."

Beatrice said, "Would it help if you spoke to Wyatt? He can be very good at helping in times like these."

Alice gave her a grateful look. "Would you mind asking him to get in touch? He does have a very good manner and he might be able to do me some good."

"Of course I will. I know he'll be happy to do anything he can."

Meadow said fiercely, "But Flossie couldn't have shown you up, Alice. You're a Dappled Hills *institution*."

This managed to elicit a chuckle from Alice. "That's sweet of you, Meadow, even if it makes me sound as old as Methuselah. And maybe the term 'show me up' was unkind of me. I always felt as if Flossie wasn't really aware of what she was doing half the time. Besides, she fell in love with the mountains here when she was visiting me about a year ago. Then she suddenly just decided to up and move over here. We have had some good times here.

I'm so *glad*, now, that we had the opportunity to spend more time together before it was too late."

"That's wonderful that you had that time," said Beatrice.

"Isn't it? I was trying to put the past behind me and move forward. Everyone thinks sisters should always be really close, but that's not always the case, is it? The truth is that Flossie was a tough person to like sometimes. There was much to *admire* about Flossie, though, and I definitely admired her. If you wanted something done, you handed the task over to Flossie. Needed someone to lead a committee? Flossie was your woman. People appreciated that she was the kind of person who could organize a mess into something that would run like clockwork. But she wasn't the easiest person to hold a conversation with. She was a very impatient person and that impatience bled through to other parts of her life."

Beatrice said wryly, "I can relate to being impatient. It's one of the traits I'm trying to get a handle on." She'd originally thought that when her life became slower after retirement that her impatience might abate. But now she was thinking the trait was deeply ingrained.

Alice said, "Good for you for trying to be more patient! I wish Flossie had been trying to do the same. She didn't always treat people the way they should be treated or the way she'd want others to treat her. I listened to Wyatt's sermon on the Golden Rule recently and was thinking about Flossie the whole time. I wish she'd been in the congregation to hear it, but of course she wasn't much of a churchgoer. I'm afraid that Flossie was especially hard on Trina Wallace lately."

Meadow frowned. "How was Flossie hard on Trina?"

Alice shook her head. "Well, Trina was all excited apparently, because she was hoping to be a quilt show circuit judge. She's in the Cut-Ups, you know. Trina had been thinking about applying for years but hadn't gotten up the courage. Then, one day, she did. She filled out the forms and asked Flossie for a recommendation letter and sent everything off. But Flossie recommended against her to the committee."

Meadow put her hand to her heart. "Oh, no."

"That's what I said when Flossie was telling me about it. Flossie said she 'did it to be kind' because she didn't think Trina would do a good job and then she'd feel like a failure. Flossie felt she'd rescued Trina from all that. But Trina became very dejected when Flossie told her. And she told Trina to her face that she didn't think she had the breadth of experience to make a good judge."

"Of course she was dejected after hearing that!" said Meadow.

Alice added, "Flossie was completely unrepentant when I told her that was an unnecessary way of handling the situation. She could simply have told Trina that she had some concerns and that it would be best if Trina found someone else to write the recommendation letter. Or Flossie could have simply told Trina that she was too busy to write one."

"But Flossie didn't think she'd done anything wrong?" guessed Beatrice.

"That's right. And, of course, she technically didn't. She *thought* she was doing the right thing. But I felt so badly for Trina that I apologized to her on Flossie's behalf." Alice shook her head. "Unfortunately, there was more trouble, too. She'd been talking about a new quilter who'd been visiting the Cut-Ups. I think her name was Jessica."

Meadow's eyes grew wide. "Our little Jessica."

Alice looked confused and Beatrice added, "Jessica is also attending some Village Quilter guild meetings, too."

Alice said dryly, "Probably because Flossie wasn't making her feel especially welcome at the Cut-Ups."

Meadow didn't say anything to this since Flossie was now departed and Meadow didn't like to speak ill of the dead. But the indignant look on her face said it all.

Alice continued, "She didn't think much of experimental approaches or modern quilts. I told Flossie if she couldn't say anything nice, not to say anything at all, just like our mother taught us. And I do think Flossie tried to just avoid Jessica for a while in order not to say anything rude about her quilting. But Jessica was determined to get the advice of an expert."

Meadow said, "Why, of *course* she was! Flossie had been a quilt show judge for ages, after all. Jessica is just starting out. Naturally she'd want to get Flossie's opinion on her work."

Beatrice hid a smile. Meadow looked absolutely horrified. But then, Meadow had always been very supportive of every quilter, even when their quilts weren't entirely to her taste.

Alice gave another sigh. "She felt someone needed to put Jessica in her place."

Now Meadow looked even more aghast.

Alice tried to explain. "She thought Jessica needed to recognize that everything wasn't just going to fall into place for her in terms of quilt shows and recognition for her work. Flossie believed that nothing beat hard work and paying your dues. She believed Jessica was looking for shortcuts or instant praise and glory." Alice held up her hands as Meadow opened her mouth in defense of Jessica. "Her words, not mine. That happened this morning and Flossie had called me on the phone afterwards because she was irritated about the whole scene. I guess Jessica must have been crushed and Flossie didn't feel guilty at all about that. She was just annoyed that Jessica wasn't grateful for her expert advice."

Meadow still looked like she wanted to explore the topic a bit more, so Beatrice hastily intervened. Although Alice might not look as if she was shattered over Flossie's sudden death, grief had a lot of different faces. "You and Flossie—it seems as if you must have been close."

Alice looked a little startled over this idea. "Does it?"

"Since Flossie was calling you so much. It sounds like she really relied on you to bounce things off of you."

Alice looked as if this hadn't occurred to her. "I suppose she did. Honestly, I feel bad about saying it, but her phone calls really stressed me out most of the time. Flossie seemed to want absolution for her awful behavior and I wasn't going to give it to her. I wanted her to try harder to be nicer. To follow the Golden Rule, like Wyatt mentioned in his sermon. I almost felt as if Flossie's calls just served to make me extremely uncomfortable around the various people she'd offended. Like she was alienating me from half the town." She sighed again. "And now I've got to think about planning her service."

Beatrice said, "Wyatt would be happy to give you a hand with that."

Alice nodded. "Something simple. I'm sure Wyatt could do these services blindfolded by now."

Meadow still looked as if she wanted to talk a bit more so Beatrice quickly added, "And now, Meadow and I should probably be going. We're glad to see that you're all right—but if you need anyone to talk with later, you have our numbers. And Wyatt's, too."

"Thank you both so much," said Alice warmly as she walked them to the door and then closed it carefully behind them.

Chapter Five

MEADOW STARTED UP THE van. "Well, that went well, don't you think?" she asked in a cheery voice as she headed them home. "I thought Alice was holding up very well, considering. Our visit definitely did her some good, too. Her color was much better by the time we left."

Beatrice made a vague sound of agreement and Meadow darted a glance across at her. "You didn't think the visit went well?"

"No, I did. But I was just thinking about what Alice was saying about her sister."

Meadow snorted. "She wasn't very happy with Flossie, but Flossie certainly deserved it. The idea of letting poor little Jessica down like that. And Jessica's quilts are *marvelous*."

Beatrice thought about this for a couple of minutes. "That's the thing—they *are* marvelous. Flossie would have known that, too, from her years of judging. Maybe they weren't Flossie's favorite *types* of quilts, but Flossie would have been able to recognize that the craftsmanship was very good."

Meadow said darkly, "Maybe Flossie was jealous. She felt envious over Jessica's natural talent. Maybe she thought Jessica, since she's so young, might eclipse us all with her quilts before long."

"Actually, that could well be the case," said Beatrice in a thoughtful voice. "It sounded like Alice thought Flossie even moved here to 'show her up' in some way, as if Flossie was a very competitive person. So maybe Flossie was envious over Jessica's natural talent and her youth. She has her whole quilting career ahead of her."

"Well, discouraging Jessica was a terrible way to go about it. She should have just politely declined to offer her opinion. Or told her that her quilts were *technically* very good and just not been overly-enthusiastic about it. She didn't have to be awful to the girl," steamed Meadow.

Beatrice said, "And now Jessica is sure to be treated as a suspect in Flossie's death."

Meadow gave Beatrice an alarmed look before quickly turning her gaze back to the road. "What?"

"It sounded as though Ramsay and the state police weren't treating Flossie's death as a natural one. That means they'll be looking for likely suspects. Unfortunately, Jessica seems as if she could be one."

Meadow glowered at the road ahead. "Ramsay better not consider her as a suspect. I'm sure Jessica must have felt crushed, but it doesn't mean she went back later and *killed* Flossie. For heaven's sake! We'll have to find better suspects for Ramsay to investigate."

Beatrice's lips tilted slightly into a smile. Meadow could be so very protective of her fellow quilters. "Whom would you suggest?"

"Well, maybe Alice. She probably stands to gain from Flossie's death, since Flossie wasn't married and didn't have any children. Plus, it sounds like she and Flossie had a tough relationship sometimes." Meadow spoke quicker as she warmed to her topic.

"Alice also mentioned Trina."

Meadow's brow furrowed dramatically as she pulled into Beatrice's driveway. "I'm sure Trina would never have considered murdering Flossie, even if she *did* send a negative recommendation letter."

Beatrice could tell that Meadow was just getting geared up in her defense of Trina. But now she was ready for a break from Meadow. Besides, it occurred to her that she was in exactly the same situation as she'd been in about this time yesterday—no idea what she and Wyatt were going to eat for supper right before suppertime. She supposed they could have the leftovers from last night, but usually they had leftovers two nights later instead of the very next day.

"I've got to run for now, Meadow. I'll talk to you later, okay?" She gave Meadow a cheery wave and hopped out of the car and into her house. Noo-noo was eagerly watching her through the front window as she walked down the stone walkway and approached the cottage.

When she got inside, she stooped down to give the little dog a cuddle. Then she went all out and sat on the floor with her back against the wall as Noo-noo happily climbed on her lap and licked at the underside of her chin.

Beatrice heard a car door and hoped it wasn't Meadow with yet more to say about suspects and Flossie. She was relieved when Wyatt came in the door, instead. He looked surprised at the sight of his wife on the floor. "Is everything okay?" he asked with concern.

"Sort of," said Beatrice with a sigh. "It's better now that I'm here with you. And Noo-noo, of course." Noo-noo nuzzled her furry head closer to Beatrice's. Beatrice rubbed her for a few moments before getting to her feet. "Did you hear about Flossie?"

Wyatt shook his head, looking confused. "We were just talking about her yesterday."

Beatrice filled him in as they walked over to the sofa to sit down. After she'd told him about the ill-fated visit to pick up quilting supplies from Flossie and their subsequent conversation with Alice, Wyatt's face grew grim. "I'm so sorry to hear that. I'll call Alice now."

He was fishing his phone out of his pocket as Beatrice added, "Oh, and I hope grilled cheese sandwiches or eggs sound all right for dinner. I somehow went the entire day without planning for eating again."

"Grilled cheese sounds good as long as I'm allowed to make them. It sounds like you've had a tough day."

"I may take you up on that," said Beatrice with relief. "I'll get out of your hair while you make your phone call."

She did want to get out from being underfoot, but mostly, Beatrice just wanted to retreat to the hammock in the backyard. It had become quite an escape for her. Noo-noo bounded along beside her as they headed outside. Sometimes Noo-noo liked getting in the hammock with Beatrice, but this time she seemed content to lie on the ground next to the hammock and take in everything around her. There was plenty to look at as the birds were having their evening meal at the feeders in the backyard. Carolina wrens, nuthatches, and chickadees were at the feeders and some larger birds like doves were cleaning up seeds underneath them. There was a light breeze playing through the trees and the cheerful chirping of the birds made Beatrice drift off to sleep.

When she woke up again, Wyatt was standing there with a tray full of food. “Feel any better?” he asked.

Beatrice nodded and stretched. “I didn’t mean to fall asleep but I feel better for having done it. Sometimes I wake up groggy and irritable from a nap but not this time.” She smiled at Wyatt. “You are amazing. Thanks for supper. And you even heated up some tomato soup to go with the grilled cheeses.”

Wyatt chuckled. “Hardly a culinary masterpiece, but it will hopefully be edible. And it was fast and easy.”

Beatrice joined him at the wrought-iron table they had on the patio. Noo-noo’s nose twitched with interest as she smelled the food. The little dog settled close by in case any crumbs fell.

They sat in a peaceful quiet for a few minutes as they ate. A blue jay squawked loudly from the feeder and then fell quickly silent when a hawk screeched overhead.

After a little while, Beatrice said, “How was Alice doing when you checked in on her?”

Wyatt took a sip of his iced tea and said, “She seemed all right. She didn’t really want to talk about how she was handling Flossie’s death. I let her direct the conversation. Alice pretty quickly moved on to the topic of Flossie’s funeral. I felt like planning the service helped by giving her something to focus on.”

Beatrice nodded. "It's nice to have tasks to knock out when life gets overwhelming. Then you can follow your to-do list and not really have to think as much. Did she make plans for the service?"

"Alice wanted me to give a simple graveside service. We're going to speak more about it when the police are in contact with her to let her know when Flossie will be released to the funeral home."

Wyatt and Beatrice had just finished up their sandwiches and soup when Noo-noo started barking and wagging her nubbin of a tail as she darted for the back door.

Beatrice raised her eyebrows. "I didn't hear anything, did you?" she asked.

"No. But she has those big ears. Maybe she heard the doorbell ring," suggested Wyatt as he stood up and headed toward Noo-noo.

But then the little dog trotted off, still woofing, for the gate leading to the side of the house.

"Anybody there?" called out Wyatt.

Beatrice sighed. Being a minister sometimes meant that one's evenings were spontaneously interrupted by folks dropping by. Wyatt never seemed to mind it, but Beatrice sometimes did. Sometimes she felt like she and Wyatt had a tough time finding time just to be alone. She tried to summon that patience she was talking about earlier . . . the patience she'd always found so elusive.

Beatrice changed her mind about the interruption when she saw Posy peeking into the backyard from the gate. "I'm so sorry," she said, looking stricken. "I didn't mean to interrupt your supper."

"We're all done," said Beatrice, gesturing to the empty plates. "We were just enjoying the nice evening outside."

Wyatt opened up the gate and Posy came inside, stooping to give Noo-noo an absentminded pat. Then she sat at the table with them, still looking a little awkward. She gave them a sweet smile, but her expression was troubled.

"Can I get you anything to eat? Or a glass of iced tea or water?" asked Wyatt politely.

Posy quickly shook her head. "No, thank you. I just . . . well, I stopped by because I'm in a bit of a quandary."

"What's wrong, Posy?" asked Beatrice, frowning.

Posy took a deep breath. "It's about Flossie. It's just that I wonder if maybe I know who killed her."

Beatrice exchanged a glance with Wyatt and both of them involuntarily leaned in closer to Posy.

Posy hesitated. "I'm afraid it will sound like gossip. But if I *don't* say anything, I'm worried Ramsay won't be able to bring the right person to justice."

Wyatt said gently, "That must be a terrible weight to bear, Posy."

Posy sagged a little as if just having someone acknowledge the fact was a relief. "It has been, all afternoon. I don't want to get anyone into any trouble, but I know I probably need to let Ramsay know."

"What happened?" asked Beatrice.

Posy answered this with a question of her own. "Do you know Gail Middleton?"

Beatrice nodded. "She's one of the Cut-Ups." She sighed at the idea that Gail could somehow be involved with Flossie's death. Meadow would be decidedly displeased about having yet another quilter implicated.

Wyatt said, "Ralph Middleton helps us out at the church a lot with computer issues and audio/visual, too. Are they doing all right?"

Posy shook her head. "Not really. At least, they could be better. Gail came in recently to the shop to get some fabric. The store was quiet and I was just chatting with her when she suddenly burst into tears. So I settled her down on the sofa and brought her some lemonade and cookies. Maisie got in her lap that that seemed to calm her down a little bit."

Maisie was the quilt shop cat and was very much a lap cat who had the extraordinary ability to give love and decrease people's blood pressure.

"Did that help?" asked Wyatt.

"Well, it made Gail stop crying, but then she got really angry."

"With you?" asked Beatrice, frowning.

"With her husband. With Ralph. She said that he was having an affair." Posy hesitated. "With Flossie."

"Ohh," said Beatrice and Wyatt in chorus.

Posy nodded miserably. "That's what's got me so worried. Gail was so mad at Ralph. But she was also really angry at Flossie, too. It sounded like she was mostly blaming Flossie for Ralph getting involved with her. What if she confronted Flossie and then somehow lost control? I really can't imagine it, but it's all I've been able to think about today."

"I think you're going to have to let Ramsay know about this," said Wyatt. "Let him sort it out and get to the bottom of it. Maybe Gail didn't have anything to do with Flossie's death at all. But it's best for the police to clear her."

Beatrice said slowly, "And, of course, the affair gives Ralph a motive, too, since he was in a relationship with Flossie. Maybe he had some sort of spat with her and something went horribly wrong."

"Ramsay will be able to speak with them both and figure out what to do," said Wyatt as Posy's face puckered anxiously.

She said slowly, "You're right. I guess I knew what I needed to do, but telling you two about it makes things a lot clearer. I'll run over there after I leave here. I need to get this off my chest or else I won't sleep a wink tonight."

Beatrice said, "Maybe you should just give Ramsay a call instead of dropping by the house. You know I love Meadow, but if you tell Ramsay anything in Meadow's presence, it has the potential to become gossip."

Posy blinked and then said, "Oh, good point. Yes, I'll just give him a call." This decided, she reached down to give Noo-noo a rub and the corgi lovingly lay her head against Posy's leg. Posy glanced at one of the birdfeeders and said, "You have some goldfinches here! They're just beautiful, aren't they?"

The next few minutes were filled with lighter talk of bird-houses, feeders, and their seasonal bird visitors.

Once Posy left, looking a lot less-worried than she had when she'd arrived, Wyatt rubbed a hand over his face. "What a mess."

"At least Posy seems like a load has been lifted from her shoulders. And for all we know, Gail and Ralph might not have had anything to do with Flossie's death. As you were saying, it's best to let Ramsay use the information to figure out if they did. I don't really know either of them very well, do you? I see Gail over in the floral department at Bub's Grocery sometimes and at the occasional quilt show, but that's about it."

Wyatt said, "I do know Ralph fairly well since he spends a good deal of time helping us at the church. He seems to be one of those people who likes staying busy. He recently retired and immediately contacted Edgenora to see if the church needed any IT help."

Beatrice said slowly, "I wonder if he's trying to spend more time out of the house and away from Gail—if that's a sign their marriage was having problems."

"It's certainly possible."

They must have both been sounding rather grim because suddenly Noo-noo put her little paws up on the edge of Beatrice's chair and looked at them solemnly as if trying to assess what was wrong. Beatrice chuckled and gently rubbed behind the corgi's ears. "It's okay. How about if we head inside and relax?"

They walked back into the house and Wyatt turned on some soft jazz music and Beatrice helped them both to some ice cream with chocolate syrup drizzled on top. Beatrice felt the stress roll off her as she picked up her book and Wyatt read alongside her on the sofa.

Chapter Six

THE NEXT MORNING, BEATRICE made a list to help give her day a little direction. She knew she needed to do some laundry and water her houseplants. For some reason, Beatrice had great success growing things outdoors, but less success with houseplants. She'd either overwater them or underwater them or put them in spots that were too sunny or too dark. She also needed to make a trip to the grocery store, considering how haphazard her meal planning had been lately. Beatrice could never seem to get onboard with meal prep, but she saw that she at least needed to have some things on hand for any last-minute meals. Wyatt had been lucky he'd even had the ingredients for grilled cheese sandwiches and tomato soup the night before.

She started the laundry, watered the plants (using a lighter hand than usual), then came up with a grocery list. Finally, she headed out for the store. When she got to Bub's Groceries, she looked at her list and sighed. It would definitely have to be the big grocery cart and not the little one. She greatly preferred the smaller one for navigating the aisles but there simply wouldn't be any room for all the things on her list.

Beatrice was just considering the avocados and wondering if they were over-ripe when she heard someone calling her name. She turned and saw Gail Middleton in the floral department, looking her way. Gail was a tall, statuesque woman of about sixty who always wore very tailored, simple clothes in muted tones.

"Hi, Gail," said Beatrice.

Gail gave her a tense smile. "Hi, Beatrice. Sorry to interrupt your shopping." She glanced around as if to ensure the store manager wasn't looking her way.

"No problem at all. Is there anything I can help you with? Beautiful flowers, by the way."

Gail's smile became softer at the compliment. "Thanks. The house plants are actually on sale."

Beatrice chuckled. "I may need to take you up on the sale if my current plants don't start looking better. I was just thinking that no matter what I do, they always look a little stressed."

Gail nodded tightly, the mention of stress perhaps reminding her of her own. "I was just going to let you know that I know you and Meadow were supposed to pick up the quilting supplies for the round robin the guilds are doing. Actually, I think you *did* try to pick them up, didn't you?"

Beatrice sighed. "That's right. Poor Flossie."

"Yes." Gail paused as if not totally sure she could remember what direction she'd been steering the conversation. She finally added, "Ramsay brought the supplies back to the Cut-Ups, and I have them in my car. You can just take them right out, if you like. Flossie had printed out the different specs for the quilt, so the directions are in there, too."

"Sure. Do you want me to just run back by the floral department when I've checked out my groceries so you can let me in your car?"

Gail said, "Oh, I never lock my car. The bag is right there in the back seat."

She looked so absent that Beatrice said, "Are you doing all right? I'm sure you must have known Flossie pretty well from the guild. It must have been a nasty shock."

Gail colored a little. "It was a shock. But mostly, I just feel sort of bad about everything. And when Ramsay brought over the quilting supplies this morning when I was about to leave for work, he asked me a lot of really pointed questions about Flossie."

Considering Posy's visit from the night before, Beatrice wasn't at all surprised to hear this. Gail lowered her voice after glancing around them again and said, "I feel like I need to talk to somebody, Beatrice. And besides being the minister's wife, you've always seemed so sensible. It's quiet in the store now and I think my manager is on his break. I was wondering if I could bend your ear for a minute." The flush deepened a bit and she added in a rush, "Unless I'm holding you up. You're obviously here to get some shopping done."

"Oh, I have a few minutes. I need to gear myself up for the produce aisle. Wyatt and I have been trying to eat healthily, but sometimes I'm overly ambitious when I'm faced with vegetables. I'll end up buying two pounds of green beans or something." Beatrice smiled, hoping to put Gail at ease.

Gail relaxed a little and said in a rush, "Thank you, Beatrice. It's just that I'm so worried. I mean, my life wasn't *perfect* before, but I was always content. You know how it is—I just sort of went through the motions and assumed everything was fine. Went to work, came home, hung out with Ralph, went to guild meetings, attended church, did some quilting. It was the same pattern but it wasn't a bad one."

"It sounds a good deal like my routines, except for the work part," said Beatrice.

Gail smiled at her. "And I'm looking forward to my retirement soon. Anyway, I noticed that Ralph seemed a little less-content than I was. He was having a midlife crisis, I guess."

Beatrice thought that unless Ralph lived until 120, it wouldn't be quite a *mid*life crisis. But she nodded, just the same.

"He got a new, sporty car. He started caring about his appearance more, which was sort of strange to me. He bought some new clothes and even started using hair products." Gail looked somewhat scandalized by this. "I couldn't imagine why Ralph suddenly cared what he looked like. He's always looked *nice*, but he wasn't spending a lot of time gazing at his reflection in the mirror. But then I realized why he cared so much."

Beatrice knew what was coming but tried to look as if she was hearing it for the first time.

Gail took a deep breath. "I followed him one day, when it was my day off. I'm not proud of that, but I had to find out what was going on. He kept telling me he was going to the church to help with the computer issues over there. At first, I was just relieved that he had something to keep him busy. I'd talked to a lot of friends who had retired husbands and complained about them being underfoot. When he started helping out at the church, I thought it was a great idea."

Beatrice said, "Wyatt was saying he'd been a big help."

"I'm glad. Ralph has always enjoyed working, so I wasn't really surprised when he decided he needed to volunteer at the church. But I was a little surprised how he was dressed up to go over there. I mean, it's one thing to dress up for a service on Sunday, but quite another to dress up to volunteer there on a Wednesday morning. Plus, it seemed like he was gone an awful lot for volunteering. I started to get suspicious so I followed him, like I said. I saw that instead of going to the church, he'd gone over to Flossie's house." Gail's face was pinched as if it pained her to say it.

"Oh, Gail. I'm so sorry."

"Thank you, Beatrice," said Gail with dignity. "It was pretty upsetting. But then I figured that maybe he'd just gone over there for some sort of errand. I tried to make excuses for what I was seeing. After all, I thought of Flossie as a friend. We weren't close or anything, but I enjoyed talking with her at guild meetings and quilt shows. That night when Ralph and I were having supper, I asked him how his day had been. I thought maybe he'd bring up Flossie and I'd find that it had been some innocent reason that he'd been over there. But he didn't say a thing."

Beatrice said hesitantly, "Couldn't he have just overlooked it? Maybe it was something so insignificant that it didn't even qualify as something to bring up." But, having spoken to Posy, she doubted this was the case.

Gail shook her head. "Well, that's what I kept telling myself. But the very next day, Flossie came by the house to see me. I was surprised, of course. But Beatrice, her manner was just awful. She acted so smug. And she told me right to my face that she and Ralph were having an affair. Not just that—she told me that they loved each other and that Ralph was planning on leaving me."

Beatrice was momentarily speechless as she tried and failed to find words. Was anyone really that brazen?

Gail continued in a bitter voice. "I felt like she and Ralph had been making a fool of me . . . like they were laughing at me behind my back. I was incredibly hurt."

"Of course you were."

Gail gave a short laugh. "Then the hurt turned to anger. I was just absolutely furious. And getting angry happened as soon as Flossie sashayed away and I started thinking about Ralph cheating on me. We've been married for over thirty years and he does *this*? After she left, I almost felt like driving over to Flossie's house, pounding on the door and having it out with her right then. Then I decided not to. I figured I'd just make a huge scene and everyone in Dappled Hills would be talking about it. So instead, I really let Ralph have it when he came home. We were both up all night, arguing with each other."

"Was Ralph apologizing? Or was he being defensive?" asked Beatrice.

"Both. He said our marriage was 'stagnant.' Stagnant! Like it was pond full of bacteria or mold or something. But then he also tried to apologize. He said he didn't want to lose me and didn't want to face the rest of his life alone. I think he also thought our grown kids would believe he'd lost his mind. We went back and forth all night long, like I said. Finally, though, I talked about leaving him and he completely changed his tune. He looked absolutely distraught. Maybe he thought I wouldn't go through with something like that. He quickly said that he would end things with Flossie. He said she was very controlling anyway and he thought the affair had run its course."

"That must have been a relief," said Beatrice.

Gail nodded. "But I was still so mad. What I should have done was to talk to you or Wyatt right away—get some counseling. But I spoke to a couple of friends instead. I think when I talked about it, it helped me to wrap my head around it and sort of normalize it enough that it didn't hurt as much."

"That's only natural, to want to talk things over."

"It is. And it would have been fine if Flossie hadn't been murdered. But now, everything is a mess." Gail absently rearranged some cut flowers in a vase. "Ramsay somehow heard about Ralph's affair with Flossie. But I guess he's a police officer, so that shouldn't be a surprise. And I should have known that secrets don't stay quiet in a small town. But the police talked to me last night while Ralph was over at the church. And cops from the state police must have talked to Ralph while he was volunteering over there. He came back looking so stressed, so worried."

"Did you talk with Ralph about it?" asked Beatrice.

Gail shook her head. "It's like there's this wall between us now. He created the wall by having the affair to begin with. But I didn't help things either by exploding at him the way I did." She looked up at Beatrice uncertainly.

"Gail, I think you were entirely within your rights to explode like that. You didn't do anything wrong. And it was only natural for you to want to talk to others about Ralph's affair. You were hurt and you were trying to absorb this huge betrayal by talking it out."

Gail rearranged the cut flowers she had just arranged a minute before. "Thank you. I was hoping you'd say something like that. But now I'm not just feeling guilty about losing my temper, I'm worried sick. I'm worried that Ramsay thinks *I* might have killed Flossie. Although I'm not sure how he could believe that—Ramsay and I went to school together, for heaven's sake! He's known me my whole life. How could he possibly think I killed someone?"

"I'm sure he's having to approach it by the book, Gail. It's just a red-tape thing."

Gail said in a brooding voice, "I guess so."

"Do you have an alibi?" asked Beatrice.

Gail shrugged. "Not really. I was here at work yesterday afternoon, but I sometimes pop out during my breaks to run quick errands. And nobody is really keeping track of where I am. Ramsay didn't seem to be especially impressed with my alibi."

"And Ralph? I know you said the two of you didn't talk about his interview with the police, but do you know where he was?"

Gail snorted. "Clearly, I've been doing a really bad job keeping up with where my husband is. I have no idea where he was yesterday afternoon." She looked blankly at the flowers in the vase. "I did try to persuade Ramsay that I'd gotten over the affair. I told him that I had been really angry at first but then decided if Flossie wanted Ralph, Flossie could have him. That I'd decided I'd wash my hands of Ralph and our life together."

"Did Ramsay seem to buy it?"

Gail shook her head. "I don't think so. I'm not that great of an actress. I did try to stick up for Ralph, though. I'm so worried they think he was involved in Flossie's death."

"Really? It seems to me that they wouldn't consider Ralph as a major suspect if he cared for Flossie. What would be the motive?"

Gail said, "Maybe they thought things didn't go well when Ralph went over to break up with Flossie."

"So Ralph ended his relationship with Flossie by murdering her?" Beatrice shook her head. "I'm not sure that adds up."

"I'm not sure what they think, but I know Ralph is so incredibly stressed out. Even though I felt that wall between us, I did try to reach out to him, but he shut me down. Beatrice, he's so worried. He needs to talk to *someone.* I was wondering if you or Wyatt could speak with him when he's over at the church. Ralph's blood pressure has always been a problem and it must be sky-high right now. I thought it might be helpful for you to reach out to him and let him talk it through."

Beatrice said, "I can try. Or Wyatt can. We're happy to try and help. I'm not sure if he's going to want to talk about it, though."

"Maybe he won't. Maybe he'll shut you down the same way he did me. But at least we'd have tried."

Beatrice said, "Gail, you knew Flossie pretty well. Can you think of anyone else—another person who had problems with Flossie—who might have been capable of hurting her?"

Gail nodded. "I've actually been spending a lot of time thinking about it because I want to divert attention away from

Ralph and me. I know someone who's been having a really hard time with Flossie. Trina Wallace."

Beatrice saw that Gail's red flush had suddenly gotten more pronounced. Was that because she felt guilty about implicating Trina? Or because she wasn't telling the truth?

Beatrice nodded. "I think I might have heard a little about that. Trina wanted to be a quilt circuit judge, didn't she?"

"Exactly," said Gail, looking relieved that she didn't have to get into the nitty-gritty details. "Trina is my friend, of course. She's a friend to everyone in the Cut-Ups. We all encouraged her and were really proud when she started filling out her application and talking about being a judge—a NACQJ. She was doing everything she could to learn and network . . . she went to regional shows and went out of her way to speak to other judges. She also did a good deal of local judging at the shows around here and the county fairs."

Beatrice said, "And she asked Flossie for help, didn't she?"

"Of course! It made the most sense. Flossie *was* NACQJ and she knew all the right people. She also knew how the process worked and what it was like to be a judge. If Flossie didn't want to give Trina a good recommendation, she should have just told her that she was sorry, but that Trina should look to someone else for a reference. That would have made Trina feel hurt, probably, but it would have been better than totally sabotaging her with her reference letter."

"Why do you think Flossie didn't recommend her? Was it personal or did she think Flossie really wasn't a good candidate?" asked Beatrice.

Gail pursed her lips. "I think it's because Flossie wanted all the glory and the specialness of being the only quilter in Dappled Hills with that honor. She wanted to do anything she could to make sure Trina didn't get to be a judge on that level. Trina is an excellent quilter and seems to be a good judge. She knows a lot about technique and is interested in different types of quilts. She'd have been the perfect NACQJ."

"How did Trina find out that Flossie hadn't given her a good recommendation? Did she just assume it because she didn't make it as a judge and had all the other qualifications?" asked Beatrice.

Gail shook her head. "That's the thing—Flossie actually *told* Trina afterward. She was so smug about it and informed her at one of our guild meetings. Can you see a pattern here? It's just the same way Flossie was with me—that she wanted to be the one to inform me about the affair. I think it made her happy to see other people's pain."

"What was Trina's reaction when Flossie told her she hadn't given her a good recommendation? I can't imagine how she must have felt."

Gail said, "She was absolutely furious. As a matter-of-fact, Trina stormed out of the guild meeting. Just picked up the quilt she was working on and left. But I thought she handled it really well. That was better than making a big scene with Flossie. As my mama always used to say, 'if you can't say anything nice, don't say anything at all.' And that's kind of the philosophy we all used to deal with Flossie for the rest of the meeting. No one really said anything to her because we were all horrified on Trina's behalf."

"Did Flossie seem chastened at all?"

"Not a bit!" said Gail. "She was gloating to herself for the rest of the meeting." She glanced behind Beatrice and started getting a bag of potting soil out. "That's my manager coming around so I better get busy. Remember to get the supplies out of my car . . . it's the old, white minivan parked in the shade."

And with that, Gail started busily repotting a plant.

Chapter Seven

BEATRICE MADE HER WAY through the grocery store a bit more distracted than she'd been at first. In fact, she was so distracted that she managed to forget half of the things she'd intended to buy. After checking out, she did pick up the quilting supplies and put them in her car. Then she called Meadow.

"Hi there. Are you at home?" asked Beatrice.

"Home?" asked Meadow as if that was a ridiculous idea. "No. I'm at the Patchwork Cottage."

"Got it. I'm going to run by with the quilting supplies from the Cut-Ups if you're going to be there a little while."

"Really? How did you manage to get those?" Meadow's voice was positively delighted and nosy at the same time.

Beatrice just wanted to discharge herself of her responsibility and not get into a long explanation on the phone. "I'll tell you once I get over there."

It was such a short distance from the grocery store to the quilt shop that Beatrice just took the bag of supplies and walked over instead of looking for parking again. By the time she opened the door, Meadow had apparently told everyone who was in the shop that Beatrice was coming over with the quilting materials that had been at Flossie's house. They all looked at her wide-eyed.

"How did you get it?" asked Meadow as if the bag were full of some sort of contraband.

"From Gail Middleton," said Beatrice. "Ramsay apparently knew the supplies were from the Cut-Ups and thought they should go to another member of the guild."

"I should have briefed him that the supplies were supposed to come to the Village Quilters," said Meadow with a sigh. "He's been so busy with the investigation that I haven't really had time to even speak with him."

Posy had given Beatrice a concerned look at the mention of Gail's name, but Beatrice shot her a reassuring smile. They definitely didn't want Meadow to get on the scent of local gossip so Beatrice quickly changed topics.

"Did I hear Tiggy might be interested in coming to our guild meetings?" This was actually a complete fabrication on Beatrice's part, but she couldn't seem to come up with another distraction on such short notice.

Meadow looked surprised. "Oh, I don't think so, Beatrice. You know how I love to have new folks in the guild. But Tiggy hasn't seemed very interested in joining up, at least permanently. She did tell me that she'd come along with Savannah or Georgia a time or two. But her nieces thought Tiggy might try to make us all eat celery sticks and hummus instead of our usual cornucopia of food."

Posy said fondly, "Tiggy appears to be a bit more interested in her sewing and knitting. Although she comes by the shop quite a bit."

"How's that coming along?" Beatrice's voice was trepidatious. She'd personally witnessed Tiggy's sewing and it was a bit slipshod.

"Actually, she's come a long way," said Posy, eyes dancing. "One of the ladies from the church wanted to host a sewing seminar a couple of weeks ago and Tiggy was in attendance. She said she learned so much."

"That's good," said Beatrice fervently. But it was still probably just as well that Tiggy hadn't decided to turn her dubious talents to doing much quilting.

"What's new at the shop?" asked Beatrice. She glanced over at a small folding table on the other side of the sitting area. "Is that a board game set up?"

Posy smiled. "*That's* what's new at the shop. It's Scrabble and the reason it's over there is because of Tiggy. She was telling me the other day that she's always been a huge fan of board games but has never had anyone to really play with."

Tiggy had been single and with no romantic partners until Dan had come around. Beatrice said, "I wonder if Dan plays games with her sometimes."

Posy nodded. "She said he does, but he has a fondness for chess, which is not Tiggy's favorite. She likes Scrabble and Monopoly and seemed so wistful that I suggested we set up a table at the shop for games."

"That's very generous of you, Posy."

Posy quickly shook her head. "Not really. I've always wanted the Patchwork Cottage to be a place for quilters to hang out and relax and visit. This helps with that goal. Because it's more fun to have our quilting be a community thing, isn't it? Like with the round robin quilt. Jessica Brennan said she'd come by in a bit, too, thinking about people coming to hang out. As a matter of fact, she should be here any minute."

"Oh, good!" said Meadow. "I was afraid that she'd give up quilting altogether, considering how discouraging Flossie had been."

Beatrice said, "Surely she wouldn't have done *that*. She has too much talent."

"Yes, but she's a young person. You and I would be irritated and defensive, but then we'd come back with an amazing quilt months later just to show Flossie she didn't know what she was talking about. Jessica is different. I think for her, it felt like a major set-back."

Posy said, "She's still interested in quilting, though. I encouraged her to come in and look through fabrics and talk with other quilters. Jessica said she needed some inspiration, and I thought that would be the best way to get it."

The bell rang and they glanced over, seeing Jessica there. Beatrice had the feeling that it might be a little intimidating having them all gaping delightedly at her, so she murmured an excuse and headed over to Posy's sitting area to give Jessica some space. Posy took the hint and greeted Jessica warmly before heading over to price some new fabric that had come in.

Meadow, naturally, didn't seem to pick up on any hint at all. She rushed over to give Jessica what appeared to be a crushing hug and exclaimed, "I'm *so* glad you're here today! Posy was just showing me some of the latest fabrics she has in. Let's take a look at them!"

Beatrice settled down in an armchair in the sitting area. Miss Sissy, a regular at the shop, was taking up a good deal of the sofa and was enthusiastically snoring. Maisie, the shop cat, was curled up against her in a ball and didn't seem to mind the snoring at all. Beatrice, however, wished she had some earbuds with her to drown out the sound.

Meadow's Tour of Fabrics went on for a few minutes with Meadow cheerfully saying things from time to time like "can't you just picture this as a lovely quilted bag?" or "this would look fabulous in a log cabin pattern, wouldn't it?"

Then Jessica and Meadow rounded the area that held notions and joined Beatrice and the still-sleeping Miss Sissy. Jessica said shyly, "Hi, Beatrice."

Beatrice smiled at her. "Good to see you today, Jessica. How are things going? Are you working on something new?"

Jessica shook her head, face clouding up a little. "Not yet. I'm kind of re-evaluating what direction I want to go in with my quilting. Sometimes it's good to sort of take stock, you know?"

Meadow knit her brows. "Only if it's *your* idea to do so. Don't let anyone else influence what you want to work on."

Meadow seemed to be warming up for a rant, so Beatrice quickly interjected, "I agree with Meadow. It's too much of a chore to work on something you don't love doing. It's a lot more fun to quilt when your project is something you're excited about."

Jessica said, "The problem is that I'm not really excited about quilting right now at all. I'm wondering if I should just take a break for a little while."

Miss Sissy glared at Jessica with steely eyes. "No!" she said.

Jessica looked confused. "Sorry?"

"No stopping quilting," said the old woman gruffly.

"You think her quilts are good too, don't you?" asked Beatrice.

Meadow exclaimed, "Of course she does!"

Miss Sissy nodded. Then she promptly fell back asleep.

Jessica blinked in surprise. Beatrice said quietly, "Being around Miss Sissy is like stepping through the Looking Glass with Alice."

Jessica chuckled. "But she *is* awesome. I loved going by her house yesterday morning to see her quilts and show her a couple of mine."

"Oh, that's right—how did that go?" asked Beatrice.

"Whoever gave me the tip to bring food was a genius," said Jessica after carefully checking that Miss Sissy was still snoring away. "When I first arrived, she gave me such a suspicious look that I wondered if I'd gotten the day wrong. But after she spotted the quiches, she opened up the door and let me right in."

"I bet she did," said Meadow, grinning. "What did you think of her quilts?"

"They were fantastic, of course—both the quilts that she made herself and the ones that were her family's quilts." She paused and said, "It was a little dark in her house, so I stepped over to the door to look at them in the light. She hissed at me and I thought for a second she believed I was going to walk out with one or two of them."

"Sounds like Miss Sissy," said Beatrice in a wry voice. "Did you show her some of your quilts, too?"

Jessica nodded. "She liked looking at them. She even found some elements in my quilts that reminded her of themes in some of her older quilts. It was nice to find a connection." Her stomach growled a little and she grimaced. "I haven't had a chance to grab anything to eat today. I wonder if Posy has any snacks out."

Meadow said, "She has some amazing chocolate chip cookies. I'll bring us a paper plate of them."

While Meadow popped off to get their snacks, Jessica said, "I swear Meadow has more energy than I do."

"And she's twice your age," said Beatrice wryly.

Jessica sighed. "It's just been a very stressful last week." Her voice dropped. "And now poor Flossie."

"It was a shock, wasn't it?" asked Beatrice.

Jessica nodded. "I couldn't believe it. I had just spoken with her, *seen* her, yesterday morning. When Carl told me the news, I thought he was making some sort of horrible joke." She gave a short laugh. Don't get me wrong—Flossie was a hard woman. But I had a lot of respect for her talent and her eye for art."

"I know just what you mean. Flossie always seemed so *vital*," said Beatrice. "Full of life, full of opinions. It's hard to imagine that she's gone. You were at home then, when you heard?"

Jessica nodded again and sighed. "After Flossie told me she didn't think much of my quilts, I went right home and cried my eyes out."

Meadow, back with the cookies, arrived in time to hear that last bit. Her eyes narrowed at the thought.

"I'm so sorry," said Beatrice.

"Thanks." Jessica took a cookie with a smile for Meadow. "I'm a lot better now. Carl reminded me that it was just one person's opinion. Besides, I'll really have to toughen up if I'm going to start seriously competing in quilt shows. *Anyway*, enough of that. I got my feelings hurt and came home and moped the rest of the day there until Carl came home from work."

"You must have been very upset with Flossie," said Beatrice. "I've heard that she was something of a straight-shooter."

"That's one way of putting it," said Meadow darkly.

"She definitely didn't sugarcoat her words. But even though I was hurt, I wasn't *angry* at Flossie. How could I be? She was just speaking the truth as she saw it."

"That's very generous of you," said Meadow hotly.

"Well, Carl helped me gain a little perspective last night. He reminded me that maybe Flossie was just a fan of more traditional quilts. Perhaps she really didn't like anything non-traditional."

"But you enjoy doing modern quilts," said Meadow.

Jessica said, "That's right. That's really where my heart is. I realized that even if it meant I may not win over judges, I want to stick with what I love doing. I guess what I really need to find out is whether I should be quilting for myself or whether I have enough talent to enter shows. I don't want to waste my time if I don't have a chance of winning any ribbons."

Miss Sissy suddenly snored loudly, startling them all and then making them smile and lightening the moment a little.

Beatrice said, "Like I mentioned, I'd love to see your other quilts. But from what I saw at the guild meeting, you certainly do have talent."

"Of *course* you do!" echoed Meadow.

Jessica said, "Part of me feels really bad to be spending so much time and energy thinking about quilting. After all, Flossie is dead. Someone murdered her. That's a lot more important. I just wonder who on earth could have done it."

Meadow sighed. "Well, she was a difficult woman, that's for sure."

Jessica said softly, "I don't think Flossie always got along with her sister very well. I saw her being disrespectful to Alice right here at the shop recently. Posy and I couldn't believe the way she was speaking to her sister. I can't help but wonder if Alice finally got fed up with being belittled."

"Belittled?" asked Meadow.

"Flossie seemed to think she was better than Alice, somehow. More accomplished or smarter or something." Jessica shrugged.

Beatrice asked, "How did Alice take that?"

"She just sort of stood there and stared at Flossie. But her eyes were steely and right then, I decided that I wouldn't ever want to be on Alice's bad side."

Meadow said, "What on earth was Flossie saying to her?"

"I don't know if I even remember anything specific. Mostly I just remember the tone Flossie was using. She was so condescending to her sister. There was just not one bit of fondness in her voice. And that's not all. I also heard Flossie arguing with Ralph in town."

Meadow, who apparently hadn't heard any of the gossip about the Gail-Ralph-Flossie love triangle, knit her brows ferociously. "Ralph Middleton? Gail's husband? Why on earth would he be arguing with *Flossie*?"

"I'm not really sure. But it looked like an argument that Ralph was trying to keep quiet. Flossie was being loud and Ralph was looking around and trying to shush her."

Meadow said slowly, "That sounds really odd."

Jessica finished her cookie and gave them a small smile. "Well, I guess I'd better be heading along. I've got to run to the grocery store and pick up some things before I head home."

Beatrice's eyes suddenly grew wide. "Grocery store!"

"Do you need to go to the store too, Beatrice?" asked Meadow.

"No, I *went* to the store. Then, when I spoke with you, I brought over the supplies and then totally forgot that I have a trunk full of groceries." Beatrice, horrified, closed her eyes.

Jessica grimaced. "Hope there wasn't any ice cream in there. It's a pretty hot day."

"No, fortunately. But there are other things. Mercy. I'm going to have to see what I can salvage." Beatrice gave a hurried goodbye to everyone and then scooted off across the street and down to Bub's Grocery before driving home.

Noo-noo was watching her from the front window as Beatrice gathered her grocery bags and brought them inside. The little dog gave her an earnest, worried look as Beatrice swiftly unpacked the groceries, sensing her unease. She salvaged the yogurts but sadly poured the milk down the drain. Her frozen goods seemed all right and the produce was fine. But she was still kicking herself for having to throw out some of the food. Which meant, of course, there would be a trip back to the grocery store sometime in the near future.

To distract herself from her irritation, she decided to take Noo-noo for a walk. The corgi gave her a big, doggy smile, eyes shining, as Beatrice got out the leash and harness. They started walking in the direction of Meadow's house, choosing the quieter direction instead of heading toward town.

She decided she'd had quite enough of Meadow for the day, so was in the process of hurrying by the house. Beatrice heard a car pulling up behind her and winced, thinking Meadow might be arriving home after some errand. But it was Ramsay and he called out to her as he got out of his police cruiser.

Chapter Eight

RAMSAY STOOPED DOWN to greet Noo-noo, who excitedly leaned up against him. Beatrice chuckled as white and sable fur got all over Ramsay's uniform. "Sorry about that. Clearly, I need to brush my dog tonight."

"Oh, that's a benefit of policing in a small town. I think I look a little more relatable if I show up with dog fur all over myself." Ramsay gave Noo-noo another few rubs and stood up. "I was wondering if you could fill me in on anything you've picked up around town about the case?"

Beatrice smiled at him. "I think you're giving me greater credit for investigating than I deserve."

Ramsay shook his head. "Not a bit. People in Dappled Hills, even though I've known them for years, still tend to freeze up a little when I talk to them officially. It's like they think I become a completely different person."

"I can imagine that." Beatrice paused. "I'm guessing you've already been told about Ralph Middleton and Flossie."

Ramsay nodded. "And thank you for persuading Posy to give me that little tidbit of information. I had no idea about that affair before she told me."

"Apparently, they did a good job of keeping it under wraps. Meadow doesn't even seem to know about it, although she does seem to be very suspicious. Jessica mentioned an argument between Ralph and Flossie, which Meadow found extraordinary."

Ramsay raised his eyebrows. "I appreciate the heads-up that Meadow doesn't know about the affair. That is indeed amazing that she's unaware of that detail. I'll be very careful not to accidentally let something slip, then."

"I suppose the only reason a couple of people know about it is because of Gail. She was really hurt, of course, and it just spilled out to a couple of people. She told me about it earlier today."

Ramsay sighed and reached down to pat Noo-noo again. "Of course she was hurt. I have to consider her as a suspect, although it's tough to even imagine her murdering Flossie. I went to school with Gail, for heaven's sake."

"She said almost exactly the same thing. I got the impression that she's really concerned that Ralph is being questioned."

Ramsay shook his head. "And he's someone else I've known for ages. I was shocked to hear that he'd been having an affair with Flossie. He and Gail got married right after they graduated from college and they've always seemed to have a happy marriage. They were sweethearts all through high school, too—he was a football player and Gail was a cheerleader. But the fact of the matter is that he was having an illicit relationship with Flossie. That could have put him in an awkward situation."

"Because he might have wanted to end the relationship and Flossie didn't want to?" asked Beatrice.

"Exactly. Maybe Ralph just snapped when Flossie said she didn't want to end it. Or maybe *Flossie* was the one who wanted to end the relationship and Ralph lashed out at her in anger because he wanted it to continue."

Beatrice nodded. "That could be. Although Gail thought Ralph's fling with Flossie was just that . . . a fling. She believes he was just having a midlife crisis and was planning on ending things with Flossie. Gail said that Flossie was the one who told her about the affair so Flossie shouldn't have had any leverage—she shouldn't have had anything to hold over Ralph's head to force him to stay in the relationship."

"As far as we know, anyway," said Ramsay morosely. "I'm starting to wonder if I know any of these folks at all."

"There are other possibilities for suspects. You might well have already learned about them from Meadow."

Ramsay snorted. "Are you kidding? The only time Meadow would tell me about a potential suspect is if she was trying to distract me from considering a quilter as a suspect."

Beatrice raised her eyebrows.

"Don't tell me. You've got some quilting suspects."

"Well, possibly," said Beatrice. "Flossie apparently had a unique talent for making people upset and that includes quilters. One of them was Trina Wallace."

"Trina Wallace," said Ramsay thoughtfully. "One of the Cut-Ups, isn't she?"

"That's right." Beatrice quickly filled him in on Trina's dashed hopes for becoming a quilt show circuit judge."

Ramsay took out a small notebook and jotted down a couple of notes, looking grim. "I can imagine Trina being upset about that. It seems really underhanded of Flossie to have sabotaged Trina's application. She could have just told Trina to find somebody else to give her a recommendation letter."

Beatrice sighed. "It would definitely have been better if she could have been more upfront about it. I haven't spoken to Trina myself, but from all accounts she was very upset about Flossie's betrayal."

"Are there any other quilters I should know about? Sounds like Flossie might have been making waves in that group."

Beatrice hesitated. "Well, there's Jessica Brennan. I'd hate to think she had anything to do with Flossie's death, though."

Ramsay snorted. "Now you're starting to sound like Meadow. Why might young Jessica be unhappy with Flossie?"

"It's sort of a similar case. Flossie had established herself as a kind of expert on quilting and that's where the problems seem to be happening."

Ramsay frowned. "*Was* she an expert?"

Beatrice nodded. "As far as I can tell, yes. But she might have had very particular tastes as a quilting judge. Judges are supposed to be impartial, of course, but it's almost impossible not to let personal preferences get in the way. It was something I was always aware of and trying to push past when I worked as a curator. Just because something wasn't to my taste didn't mean it wasn't worthy of display. Others might enjoy it a lot more."

"I'm guessing Jessica asked Flossie for advice?"

Beatrice said, "More like her opinion. Jessica is somewhat new to quilting and is very interested in non-traditional quilts. She was interested in finding out what Flossie thought of her quilting."

"And Flossie apparently wasn't impressed?"

"No. Jessica was pretty despondent over that and even seemed to be reconsidering whether she wanted to continue quilting or not."

Ramsay frowned. "Flossie must have been harsh."

"I think being harsh was her stock in trade," said Beatrice dryly.

"Anybody else I should know about?" Ramsay was sounding decidedly grim.

"Well, there's Flossie's sister, of course," said Beatrice. "It sounds as if their relationship was a challenging one at times."

"I can imagine. I spoke to Alice immediately, of course, to let her know about Flossie. She was fairly quiet, which could have been because she was shocked by the news. But I got the impression Alice and Flossie likely weren't the fondest of each other. Did you hear about any sort of specific incident between the two of them?"

"I heard that Flossie's attitude toward Alice could be very condescending—belittling, actually, even in public. Alice believed Flossie moved to Dappled Hills to show her up in some way—be the more-important, more-successful sister."

Ramsay nodded. "I can see that. From what I saw, Flossie seemed to be a perfectionist in lots of ways. Her house was organized just so and I could tell it had been thoughtfully decorated. She was clearly ambitious, from what I've heard about both her career and her retirement goals. I'd think that might cause a little envy and friction between the two of them."

Beatrice asked, "I was wondering if your forensics team has found out exactly when Flossie died."

"Pretty much. At least, we know it was right around the time she was found." Ramsay stopped again to give Noo-noo a rub. "Well, I suppose I should let you go now. Noo-noo is ready to continue with her walk, I'm sure."

"Before you leave, how is everything *else* going?" asked Beatrice. "Is your writing going well?"

Ramsay perked up at the mention of his beloved hobby, which gave him the break he needed from the pressure of law enforcement. "It is, actually. I've been invited by a group of authors to contribute to an anthology. I've started writing a science fiction piece that I hope they'll accept for it."

"I didn't realize you even wrote science fiction," said Beatrice in surprise.

"I don't. But I do read quite a bit of it, which helps. I like a lot of the old stuff—Ray Bradbury, for instance. I've always been amazed at the amount of character development he could add to a short story. Anyway, my own story was coming along well until this case popped up. I've still got plenty of time to submit it, so it's not that much of a problem—it's just that I miss my writing time. I wish I had a little more time to read, too. I'm enjoying the book you recommended—*The Name of the Rose*."

"Isn't it marvelous? I thought you might appreciate a mystery that was historical fiction," said Beatrice. "It sort of meshes your crime investigating background with your interest in history."

"I do really like it. And I'm going to get back to reading it just as soon as I can," said Ramsay in a fervent voice. "It will be extra added motivation to solve this case."

"Are you still writing poetry?" asked Beatrice.

Ramsay sighed. "Well, I'm not writing anything right now because of the case, of course. But when I have a chance, I'm still doing some scribblings here and there." He paused. "Actually, I tried to contact literary agents for the poetry I'd written. It was quite an exercise in humility."

Beatrice winced. "Sorry. I bet it's hard to publish poetry."

He chuckled. "It certainly seems to be. I got about a hundred rejections. Before I started that process, I didn't even realize there were that many literary agents out there. It made me think that maybe I could self-publish my poetry—you know, create a little chapbook. It might be good to have something to hand down to Ash and Will." He shrugged, suddenly looking a little embarrassed.

Beatrice said warmly, "I think that's a great idea."

Ramsay gave her a grateful look. "Do you? I mean, the poetry is satisfying just from a creative standpoint, but I've always thought about it as something I wanted to share. Maybe that's the way to do it. Besides, I need something to keep myself busy."

"I'd think you were busy enough right now," said Beatrice, raising her eyebrows.

"Oh, I am, believe me. But sometimes it's good to have something to do that gets me out of the house. I like to go to the library and write. Especially when Meadow starts in on one of her special projects. This spring cleaning she's starting up is going to kill me."

Beatrice grinned, remembering how Meadow was inspired to clean. "But you get to have a wonderful, clean house to enjoy."

"That's true. And it's not that I don't appreciate her hard work and . . . vigor. It's just that sometimes it means a lot of conflict."

"Conflict?"

"Conflict within myself. I'm torn between getting as far away as possible from the sound of the vacuum and being right there with her to protect my stuff. She seems to find some of my treasures disposable." Ramsay gave her a rueful look. Beatrice could only imagine the bits and pieces that Ramsay, who was very much a packrat, might label as a treasure.

"At least her ankle is all better," said Beatrice. "Remember how antsy she was when it was broken?"

Ramsay gave a glum nod. "I think she was spending all her time dreaming about the spring-cleaning project and how she was going to attack it when she felt better." He looked almost fondly reminiscent of the days when Meadow had been less of a powerhouse. "Then she had some bills fall through the cracks and it provided an extra dose of motivation."

Ramsay sighed, said goodbye, and headed off to the house and Beatrice started to walk back down the quiet street. But then she decided to turn around. "Let's go see Wyatt, Noo-noo."

The little corgi wagged her nub of a tail at the mention of Wyatt and they set off in the direction of the church. Sometimes Beatrice and Noo-noo would walk over to see Wyatt at lunch or to escort him back the short distance to the cottage. Usually, she'd text Wyatt when she got to the church to find out if he was in his office or in a meeting with the church elders, or even on the church campus at all . . . sometimes she'd miss him altogether because he'd be visiting a member of the congregation at a retirement home or hospital.

Now, however, as Beatrice and Noo-noo approached the church, she saw Wyatt standing in the parking lot and soberly listening to whatever Ralph Middleton was saying. She hesitated, not wanting to interrupt what looked like a private conversation. But then, both men motioned her over.

Chapter Nine

THE FIRST THING SHE noticed was that Ralph seemed exhausted. His handsome features looked gray. He was a tall man with a head full of white hair and was about sixty-five years old. Ordinarily, he had a twinkle in his eyes and was lighthearted and cheerful. Now, though, there were lines of strain on his face.

"Hi Beatrice," he said politely.

"Good to see you, Ralph."

Wyatt said, "Ralph was just speaking with me about some worries he had. He told me he'd like your opinion, too."

"I'm happy to give it, if you think it will help," said Beatrice.

Ralph nodded. He cast his eyes toward the asphalt of the parking lot. "I'm ashamed to say it, but I strayed from Gail. I had an affair." He took a deep breath. "I know I've messed up and I want to do everything I can to try and fix my marriage and make our relationship work. I really screwed up. Beatrice, have you spoken with Gail at all?"

"I have, actually." Beatrice hesitated, not wanting to reveal any confidences.

Ralph said eagerly, "Did she say anything about getting back together with me?"

"Not specifically, but she was certainly concerned about you and your well-being," said Beatrice.

"Are you still living at home?" asked Wyatt.

Ralph said, "I'm at the house still, but Gail has temporarily moved in with her mother. At least, I *hope* it's just temporary. It's good to hear that she might have been worried about me." Then he frowned. "Why *was* she worried about me?"

Beatrice said, "She was concerned that the police were going to consider you a suspect because of your relationship with Flossie."

Ralph colored at the mention of Flossie's name. "Yes. Well, she's right to be concerned. From what I can gather, Ramsay and the state police certainly do think I'm a suspect."

Wyatt said quietly, "What have the police been saying?"

Ralph gave a quick shrug. "Mostly that they think I was angry with Flossie for leaking word of our relationship."

Wyatt frowned. "Flossie was telling people about your affair?"

"That's right." Ralph studied the asphalt again before looking up, that tiredness in his eyes again. "She wasn't happy that I was planning on ending our relationship so she decided to tell Gail we were having an affair. Flossie figured that Gail would get angry and leave me and then I'd end up with Flossie."

Beatrice felt this was very flawed thinking on Flossie's part.

Ralph seemed to read her thoughts. "It sounds warped, doesn't it? But Flossie always liked being in control and she figured this would put the ball in her court. But the truth of the matter was that it made me furious. I know I messed up, but it was never my intention to hurt Gail or have her find out about my infidelity. I was totally appalled when Gail told me what Flossie had done."

Wyatt asked, "How did Flossie originally act when you told her you were ending your affair?"

Ralph shifted a little on his feet, considering this. "Now, I'm not so sure. At the time I told her, she got really quiet and told me I needed to leave her house. I left the house and thought that it had been an uncomfortable scene, but that Flossie would ultimately accept the end of our relationship. She was always a very practical woman. I couldn't imagine her trying to continue a relationship that was totally over."

Beatrice and Wyatt stayed quiet and Ralph sighed. "I never should have gotten involved with Flossie to begin with."

"What happened?" asked Beatrice quietly.

Ralph shrugged again. "I don't know. I was the one who pursued Flossie and I guess I was flattered when she seemed interested in return. I've never been unfaithful during our marriage before. Not to make excuses, but sometimes I've been feeling lonely in our relationship. Gail is always so involved with things—clubs and work and volunteering—and I'm not involved with the same stuff. We just sort of drifted apart." He held up his hands. "Like I said, I don't want to make excuses. I was totally at fault here."

"Did you and Flossie have a lot in common?" asked Beatrice.

"I'm not sure that we actually did. Not nearly as much as Gail and I do, anyway. It was more that Flossie was just *different*. She was really well-read and liked to talk about international news and politics and whatever book she'd just read. She had lots of opinions about things and seemed like she'd traveled a lot and done a lot. I was impressed with everything she'd seen and learned. But she had a really hard, tough edge to her." He looked at Beatrice. "Wyatt was saying that you retired some time ago. Have you had problems adjusting to retirement like I am?"

Beatrice said wryly, "I have the feeling I'm still trying to adjust. The problem I've always had is that I have a tough time sitting still. I *want* to read my book. I *want* to relax. But it hasn't been something I'm programmed to do."

"You're doing a much better job at it," said Wyatt with a smile.

Beatrice gave him a smile. "Because I've been working on it. And because you're a relaxed person who can sit and focus on a book or a crossword for a while and I'd like to be able to sit quietly in the same room with you." She turned again to Ralph. "It sounds like you were smart to fill your extra time with volunteering. I know everyone at the church has appreciated it." She carefully left out that he'd also filled his extra time with an extramarital affair.

Ralph said, "I needed something to do. Like you said, I'm used to being busy. My friends are all settled in their own activities because they retired before I did. I never even felt like I *wanted* to retire—I kept on working when I was offered early retirement because I enjoyed it. Maybe I even found some of my identity in it. Obviously, too much time on my hands can lead to trouble for me. And now I'm entangled in a police investigation."

Wyatt's brow wrinkled. "Did you have a good alibi to give the police?"

Ralph looked uncomfortable. "Not really. I was home with Gail, trying to persuade her to take me back. I was telling her that the affair was over and I was never going to see Flossie again. The police didn't seem to think Gail was a great alibi."

"You sound like you knew Flossie pretty well. Can you think of anyone who might have wished to harm her?" asked Beatrice.

"That's really all I've been thinking about—who might have done this. If the police get a better suspect, they'll stop focusing on me. And, I guess, Gail," he added miserably.

"The police are questioning Gail?" asked Wyatt.

"Yes. And that makes me feel awful. The only connection Gail has to Flossie's death is through me. But because I made a mistake, she's considered a suspect. They think she has a motive." Ralph rubbed his forehead as if it hurt.

Beatrice said, "When you were mulling over who might be a suspect, did you come up with any valid options?"

"Maybe. Like I said, Flossie was a tough woman to get along with. She was definitely someone who knew her own mind and wasn't afraid to share what was on it. I wouldn't be surprised if her sister got mad at Flossie and did her in."

Wyatt said, "I thought I'd heard that Flossie moved to Dappled Hills to be closer to her sister."

Ralph snorted. "Maybe Flossie said that because it sounded good. The truth was that she moved to Dappled Hills because it caught her fancy when she came down here for a visit with Alice. Plus, I think it appealed to her to upstage her sister a little bit. They had a very competitive relationship—due, in no small part, to Flossie. It always sounded to me like Flossie looked down on Alice for being unambitious and for having a contented, quiet life. I think Flossie was secretly jealous at how happy Alice was. Flossie always seemed restless and on-edge to me. Part of her, maybe even subconsciously, might have wanted to stir things up and mess up some of that complacency."

From what Beatrice had heard of Flossie, this certainly sounded like a possibility.

Ralph glanced at his watch. "Well, I'd better let you go. Your little dog is definitely ready to finish her walk, I'm sure. I really appreciate the two of you talking this through with me—it's helped me to clear my brain a little. Now I know I've got to focus on getting my head back on straight and convincing Gail to come back to me. Wyatt, I might call you to make a counseling appointment if I can get Gail to agree."

Wyatt nodded. "Of course. Just let me know."

They started slowly walking back to the cottage with Noo-noo as Ralph drove away.

"Did that conversation come out of nowhere, or did he call to ask to speak with you?" asked Beatrice.

"He and I were both coming out of the church at the same time and he walked right over," said Wyatt. "He has a lot on his mind."

"I'll say." Wyatt was always more generous than Beatrice was, so she decided to keep to herself the phrase that had come to her mind: *Oh, what a tangled web we weave, when first we practice to deceive.*

There was a quick honk of a horn behind them, making Beatrice jump. "What now?" she muttered ungraciously.

Wyatt turned and said, "It's Dora Tucker."

Wyatt and Beatrice moved off the road a bit and Dora drove up next to them and rolled her window down. Her frizzy hair was standing on end as if she'd run her fingers through it and she had a very determined look on her face. But she wore that expression quite often since Dora was in charge of just about everything that needed a leader in town, aside from politics. She graced nearly every committee, every planning board, every group project of any kind.

"How are you, Dora?" asked Wyatt. Ever the gentleman, he didn't point out that Dora was clearly less-than-fine.

"Ugh," said Dora. "Things are not going well. They're not going well at all." Her gaze shifted to Beatrice. "You know all about Flossie, I'm guessing."

Beatrice said cautiously, "Well, I wouldn't say I know *all* about her, no. Of course I know about her passing."

Dora gave her an impatient look. "You know what I'm talking about. You're unofficially figuring out what's going on with Flossie's death, aren't you?"

Beatrice opened her mouth to object to this but Dora immediately cut her off. "You need to, if you're not. Like it or not, you seem to have some sort of talent for getting to the bottom of things. And I need you to take it on because the police think I had something to do with Flossie's death." Dora spat out the words as if they tasted bad in her mouth.

"I'm sure they're just doing their jobs. They couldn't possibly think you murdered Flossie."

Dora frowned ferociously at her. "They certainly can. From what I can tell, they're strongly considering the possibility that I argued with Flossie over arrangements for the regional quilt show, somehow became enraged, and then went to Flossie's house later in a homicidal state and attacked her."

"Did you argue with Flossie?" asked Wyatt.

"Pfft. Of course I did. Flossie had some absolutely absurd ideas for the regional show and I had no intention of ruining the event just so she could feel like an important part of the planning process. But I sure wouldn't endanger my life and liberty by coming at Flossie later and killing her," scoffed Dora.

Beatrice agreed. It was much closer to Dora's style to simply make Flossie's life miserable by telling her how silly her ideas were for the next decade. "What kind of ideas did Flossie have for the show?"

Dora made a face. "Unbelievable stuff. You'd think she'd never been to a quilt show in her life instead of having gone to dozens of them. She wanted a three-day quilt show. Fine. But the facility wasn't open on Sundays. So I suggested just a Friday and Saturday show. After all, traffic for the second day always drops off."

Beatrice nodded. "I've noticed that. It's not totally dead, but it's not as busy as the first day."

"*Precisely*. But Flossie decided, in all her wisdom, that we should have it open for Thursday, Friday, and Saturday. Thursday? Most folks are working or doing other things on a Thursday. And then there was the food."

Beatrice raised her eyebrows. Wyatt said, "Uh-oh. Messing with the food sounds like trouble."

Beatrice chuckled. "The food is often one of Wyatt's favorite parts of the show and I don't think he's the only one. What was Flossie saying about the food for the show?"

"She wanted to *ban* it. Can't you imagine? Everyone counts on June Bug's delicious pastries at the show. And we always have snacks there. We'd have a bunch of people show up for the show hungry and expecting to buy food at the venue."

Wyatt said, "Why didn't Flossie want food there?"

"Oh, some sort of paranoia involving protecting the quilts. We've offered food at our shows for ages and never had a problem because we have a special seating area with tables and chairs. No one is wandering around with drinks and food and looking at the quilts. Besides, we get money from the food vendors, too. It's another source of income." Dora still looked steamed at the memory. Then she shook her head as if trying to clear it. "Anyway, I went off on a tangent there. Will you do it, Beatrice? Will you try to find out what happened to Flossie?"

Beatrice said, "I'm not sure how much I can do, Dora, but I'll ask around a little."

"I don't think you even *have* to ask around. I think people like to come over and talk to you. You're fairly sensible. And it probably doesn't hurt that you're the minister's wife. That means you pretty much *have* to be a good listener. It's expected."

Wyatt hid a smile.

"I'll see what I can do, Dora."

"Good," said Dora with a sniff. "All right, see you later."

And with that, she was gone.

Beatrice muttered, "Let's get home as fast as we can before anyone else tries to talk to us."

"You know that you don't have to be some sort of proxy counselor just because you're married to me, right?" Wyatt looked searchingly at Beatrice.

Beatrice sighed. "Well, she's not really wrong. I can't blow people off like I did before I married you."

"I don't remember you blowing people off," said Wyatt.

"That's because you always prefer to think the best of me. The fact of the matter is that I'm something of an introvert. I do like avoiding people sometimes—not because I don't like them, but because I want to protect my personal time and space. Honestly," said Beatrice with a small frown, "Now that I think about it, it's likely *good* for me to be put in the position where I'm listening and advising people. My natural inclination is to isolate myself, which may not be very healthy."

Wyatt smiled at her. "That's a very generous way of looking at it."

"I'm never going to be a natural at it like you are, though."

They walked up their driveway and Wyatt reached out for her hand. "But you didn't choose the life that I chose."

"Hm. I'm not sure that's entirely true. I should have guessed what I might be in for. At any rate, I'm going to try to embrace it."

"Sounds very sensible," said Wyatt with a smile. "Just like Dora said."

Chapter Ten

THE NEXT COUPLE OF days were thankfully quieter. Despite Beatrice's promise to Dora to do some investigating, nothing really fell right into her lap. She didn't happen into anyone at the quilt shop or the grocery store. Instead, she found herself tidying up around the house, doing some reading, and catching up on her quilting project. Noo-noo also was the beneficiary of quite a few long walks.

Wyatt and Alice met a couple of times to plan Flossie's funeral and finally the day had come for the service. Alice had decided on a simple graveside funeral, apparently being kind of leery about celebrating Flossie's life too much, considering the circumstances. Beatrice arrived at the cemetery early with Wyatt and was glad that she had when an unexpectedly large crowd showed up for the service. Alice had been in Dappled Hills a long while, and the townspeople were nothing if not loyal.

There was a soloist from the church who did a lovely job singing the Lord's prayer and Wyatt delivered a short homily. At the end of the service, Alice stood to address everyone. In a tremulous voice she said, "Thanks to everyone for coming and supporting me by attending Flossie's funeral. Although Flossie was new to Dappled Hills, she spoke often of how she immediately felt as if she was accepted by the town. She felt like she'd lived here for years. I'm so grateful for that."

The soloist sang Psalm 23 and then Wyatt gave a benediction and the service wound to a close. A line quickly formed of people wanting to speak with Alice so Beatrice hung back, waiting for it to dissipate a little. As she did, she saw that she wasn't the only one—Trina Wallace was waiting right beside her.

"Hi Trina," Beatrice said.

Trina turned to give her a smile. She had graying red hair, wore a perennially serious expression, and was in her mid-fifties. Beatrice thought of her as another quilter who was good at organizing things and dedicated to what she did. She wondered if Trina and Dora Tucker got along well together in the Cut-Ups.

"How are you doing, Beatrice?" She gave a short laugh. "I guess we could both be better, considering we're at a funeral right now."

"Oh, I'm doing fairly well. I feel bad for poor Flossie, of course. How are the Cut-Ups holding up?" asked Beatrice.

Trina said, "Well, we're all shocked, naturally. I'm not saying Flossie couldn't be hard to handle sometimes, but the fact that someone murdered her is simply unbelievable." She shook her head. "Aside from that, I guess I'm doing all right. I'm looking to retire in the next few months."

There seemed to be something of an epidemic of early retirement, Beatrice reflected. First Ralph, now Trina. Her surprise must have registered on her face because Trina said, "I know I'm a little young for retirement, but I've been good about putting away money from every paycheck."

"You're in insurance, aren't you?" asked Beatrice.

"That's right. For far too long. I've always found it a tedious job and I've never taken much pleasure in it. Once I realized it wasn't really the business for me, it was really too late to try and change to a different career. I put the hours in and was a dedicated employee of course, but my heart was never in it. My real love has always been quilting."

Beatrice said, "Then you must be very excited to have more time to devote to the craft."

"I am," said Trina. "But I'm hoping to take my involvement with quilting a little further than that, too. I'd like to do some judging, as well."

This wasn't a surprise to Beatrice, but she contrived to have a surprised expression on her face anyway. "That's great, Trina. I'm sure you'll be wonderful as a quilt show judge."

Trina gave her a wry look. "That's apparently a matter of opinion." She glanced around them to ensure they were still by themselves. They were, and the line in front of Alice was just as long. "Flossie, for one, didn't think that I'd be much of a judge."

"Didn't she?"

"No. In fact, I'd asked her for a recommendation letter. I was trying to be a quilt show circuit judge, you see."

More information that Beatrice wasn't supposed to already know. "I see. So you were aiming higher than just judging the odd fair event or local quilt show."

"Exactly. Flossie and I had always gotten along perfectly well and I thought a reference from her would really mean something to the committee. After all, Flossie had been a circuit judge, herself."

Beatrice said, "And Flossie told you she couldn't give you a good recommendation?"

Trina snorted. "I wish! No, she told me she *would* give me a reference and then proceeded to give me a rotten one without my knowing." Trina shook her head. "But then, Flossie always knew her own mind and went her own way."

"That must have been a horrible surprise."

"It was. But I should have thought it through better. I should have asked Flossie if she could give me a *good* recommendation. Flossie was many things, but she wasn't a liar. She'd have told me right out of the gate that she wouldn't be able to provide that. And I'd have found someone else to give a recommendation. Meadow or someone like that."

Beatrice smiled at the type of reference letter Meadow would give a fellow quilter. She'd be positively rabid in her praise.

Trina continued, "Honestly, though, I didn't have any hard feelings against Flossie. She was trying to be a queen bee; I get that."

"Queen bee?"

Trina nodded. "She didn't want anyone else in Dappled Hills to share the spotlight with her. Flossie wanted to be the final authority on judging. I ended up feeling a little sorry for her—sorry she wasn't more willing to engage with the quilting community or give back to it. She wasn't secure enough in her own skin to let someone else shine. To me, that means Flossie had a deep-rooted insecurity and really needed to seek out the spotlight. But her world would have been a lot richer if she could have just opened up a little bit."

"That's very kind of you to look at it that way," said Beatrice. "I can't imagine how I'd feel in your shoes. Betrayed, I suppose."

"Oh, I was genuinely crushed when Flossie sent that note off to the judges. I had no idea she was going to do something like that, of course. I remember that Flossie's eyes narrowed for a second when I asked her but then she said she'd be happy to write a recommendation. Like an idiot, I believed her. I'd have never even known what she sent if she hadn't told me herself."

"What did she say when she told you?" asked Beatrice.

Trina gave a short laugh. "That she didn't think I was 'ripe enough' to be a judge. That I hadn't had enough experience to be a good one. And she told me in the middle of a guild meeting." She shook her head. "I'm not going to say it wasn't frustrating or a setback. But I'm planning to persevere and continue networking. I'll apply again."

"Good," said Beatrice. "I think you should." She paused. "Do you have any idea who might have been upset enough with Flossie to harm her? I suppose you weren't out and about near Flossie's house where you could have seen anything?"

"Unfortunately, no. I worked late that night. I had some red tape-type stuff at work that I'd been putting off and decided to go ahead and knock it out. But I have been wondering who might have harmed Flossie." She sighed and lowered her voice. "Not many people know about this, but Flossie was having an affair with Ralph. Gail Middleton's husband."

Beatrice carefully kept her features neutral. "Ah."

"Gail is a friend of mine, so she told me about it as soon as she found out. I feel awful talking about this, but I'm not sure what to do. Gail found out about the affair from *Flossie*. Can you believe it? To me, it showed the same sort of pattern that I'd seen before . . . when Flossie told me about the recommendation letters. It was like Flossie took pleasure in seeing us upset. Anyway, I've never seen Gail so angry. She was literally shaking with fury when she told me about it."

"Fury at Ralph? Or fury at Flossie?" asked Beatrice.

"Oh, I'm pretty sure at both. But she was especially angry with Flossie. Again, it was like a betrayal. Flossie was a member of our quilting guild. She was, allegedly, a friend of ours who should be looking after us. Instead, she was doing her best to hurt us in the worst possible ways. I do know that Gail blamed Flossie for the affair, though. She told me that."

Beatrice said, "She thought it was Flossie's fault that Ralph cheated on her?"

"That's right. She said that Ralph was especially vulnerable right now because of his midlife crisis."

Beatrice reflected again that Ralph was awfully old for a midlife *anything*.

Trina shrugged. "Gail thought Flossie had seen Ralph was feeling low and took advantage of it. She tempted Ralph into the relationship. Gail has always had a little bit of a temper, but nothing like murdering someone. I told her to try to put the affair behind her or get a separation to give her time to think. Or even speak with a counselor who might be able to help her decide how to approach Ralph's infidelity. Gail was really dwelling on it; she couldn't think about anything else."

"Do you think she'll ever go back to Ralph?" asked Beatrice, thinking of the conversation she'd just had with Ralph. He'd seemed so hopeful to reconcile with Gail.

"Well, they've always been together, and I can't imagine Ralph is the kind of person who's ever cheated before. But now Gail is starting a totally different life apart from him. She's moved into her mom's house. We're all in sort of advanced years to be living a radically different life than we have been. I think she'll see that they belong together. They'd always seemed to get along pretty well as a couple. They had a nice yin and yang."

Trina looked over at Alice and said, "Looks like the crowd is thinning out some. I'd better run up and speak with Alice. Good talking to you, Beatrice."

Beatrice watched as Trina walked up to the funeral tent and stood in a short line to speak with Alice. Ramsay and Wyatt were talking with each other now, both looking rather serious. She was so engrossed in watching the people under the funeral tent that she didn't notice Meadow approaching from the side until she was suddenly hugged, which startled her.

"Meadow," gasped Beatrice.

"Oh, sorry. I didn't mean to scare you."

"There's nothing like someone suddenly grabbing you at a funeral," said Beatrice in a wry voice.

"Did you think it was the Grim Reaper himself?" asked Meadow with a chuckle. "No, it's just me. But I did want to hear how things were going. Including your talk with Trina Wallace. Is she just as furious about the recommendation letter as we expected?"

"Well, she's here at Flossie's funeral, so she couldn't be too angry with her. When I was speaking with her, she did seem indignant but she wasn't exactly foaming at the mouth or anything. It did certainly appear to have hurt her feelings and pride, but Trina is resolved to keep trying to become a circuit judge."

"Good for her!" said Meadow, beaming. "I'm glad she's not letting a little thing like Flossie's opinion—or jealousy, or whatever it was—get in the way of her becoming a judge. I hear from Posy that Jessica is also doing some quilting so she seems to be working past her own setback, too."

"Do you think Trina might end up becoming a judge? Despite the negative recommendation, I mean. I'm not too familiar with the process."

Meadow considered this for a moment and then said judiciously, "I believe she will, yes. That's mostly to do with Trina herself. She's always been a hard worker and always very serious. She was the younger sister of a friend of mine, growing up. I'd go over to hang out at my friend's house to watch TV or whatever. Trina would be studying or practicing the piano or something."

Beatrice raised her eyebrows. "Self-directed practice? I mean, were her parents on her to practice the piano or was she doing it herself?"

"Oh, *she* was the reason she was practicing, no doubt about it. That's just the sort of person she was. Self-driven with lots of initiative. My friend always said that Trina would show her up constantly with better grades and trophies for things. I'd always thought she'd end up being a doctor or a nuclear physicist or something. Not that there's anything wrong with insurance work, but I just never got the sense that Trina had found her purpose in her work. I figured she just settled on something and then kept showing up every day because she was just that diligent."

"Maybe her purpose has always been quilting," said Beatrice.

"Exactly! That's what I've always thought. She needed to have a day job to support her quilting. And she does make some really stunning quilts."

Beatrice said, "I wonder if she still plays the piano. The church could use a substitute pianist from time-to-time."

"Knowing Trina, she probably still practices every day. She's pretty routine-driven." Meadow squinted across the cemetery. "Oops. Looks like my ride is about to leave. I'd better head on. See you later."

And Meadow scooted off to join Ramsay at the car.

Beatrice's own ride was going to be quite a while, as was the way with ministers at funerals. She'd speak with Alice before she and Wyatt headed home, she decided. There were still a few people clustered around her and Alice was beginning to look tired. She spotted Edgenora, the church secretary, heading in her direction and raised a hand in greeting.

Edgenora looked grim, but then she always looked very serious. She was in her late-fifties with steel-gray hair, a lean build, and almost frightening efficiency. She sat down next to Beatrice on the bench and they chatted for a couple of minutes about church-related things. Beatrice brought up Trina's possible piano playing ability and Edgenora carefully made a note in a small notebook she kept in her purse for such occasions. Beatrice once again was grateful that the church had found such a good administrative assistant. For a while, Beatrice had operated as the stop-gap secretary, and she was fervently happy those days were over.

"Well, it was a lovely service," said Edgenora, glancing back over at the tent near Flossie's grave. "It's a shame about the circumstances, of course. Flossie was taken too young."

"Mm," said Beatrice in agreement.

Edgenora said, "Although I have to say that Flossie could be a difficult woman. She certainly didn't deserve this fate, but I can see where she might get on the wrong person's bad side."

"I didn't realize you knew her," said Beatrice with surprise.

"Not very well and mostly through Dora Tucker, who'd talk about her. Flossie wasn't involved at the church for a while, but she was starting to put out feelers about becoming a member. Dora said that Flossie could be very condescending and tried to make everyone adopt her own methods for anything she was involved with."

"She wasn't a team player?" asked Beatrice.

"Not a bit. That does work for some people—folks like someone to come in and take charge sometimes. Maybe there was a committee that didn't have much direction and Flossie would come in and get things done. Considering she hadn't lived in Dappled Hills very long, it sure seemed like she settled in quickly, rolled up her sleeves, and got to work. That part made me admire her."

"But there were other things that were less-admirable about Flossie?"

Edgenora nodded. "Sometimes Flossie rubbed people the wrong way. Especially people like Dora Tucker."

"Well, Dora definitely likes doing things her own way. Usually, everyone just gets out of Dora's way and lets her work her magic. Dora is so focused and dedicated that she can take the place of two volunteers on a project."

"True," said Edgenora. "The problem was that Flossie wasn't about to let Dora just work her magic. There was definitely a lot of friction between those two. And sometimes, I thought Dora seemed just a mite wilted after being around Flossie."

"Wilted?" Beatrice tried in vain to envision this. All she could see was Dora's frizzy hair bristling with the energy that came off the woman in waves.

"Yes. That's how I thought of it, anyway. Her spirit was dampened by Flossie's pushy behavior and take-charge style. Flossie had just started getting involved with the church where she hadn't before. She came by the church office and was asking me about different opportunities to serve. Dora was there and she looked absolutely horrified. I was genuinely worried that Dora was going to start refocusing her volunteering in other areas . . . she started doing lots of volunteering for the town, I noticed. I thought she was trying to avoid Flossie." Edgenora dipped her voice even lower although there was no one remotely within earshot. "You don't think Dora could have had anything to do with Flossie's death, do you?"

Beatrice said in a comforting voice, "I really doubt it, don't you? That doesn't seem to be Dora's method of dealing with conflict. It sounds to me from what you've said that she was avoiding trouble instead of seeking it out. Besides, Dora recently asked me if I could try to figure out what was going on with Flossie's death. She was concerned that the police might consider her a suspect. That doesn't sound like the behavior of someone who has something to hide." Although there was that argument between Dora and Flossie that she and Piper had witnessed. Beatrice decided to keep that information to herself.

This made Edgenora look a bit more cheerful. "That's true. Good. Thanks, Beatrice—you've helped relieve my mind." She looked at her watch. "And now I should be heading back to the church office. I have a few things I want to wrap up there today before I call it a day."

Chapter Eleven

THE REMAINING PEOPLE at the service finally drove away and Beatrice walked back up to join Wyatt and Alice. Alice gave her a weary look and Beatrice reached out to give her hand a squeeze. "You must be exhausted."

Alice nodded, the strain showing on her features. "It's just been a long day. And I've had a lot of mixed feelings that I need to figure out how to process."

Wyatt said, "You did a wonderful job here today, though. Now you can go home and put your feet up for a while. Funerals can be incredibly draining."

"The service was beautiful," offered Beatrice. "It was a lovely tribute to Flossie."

"Thanks to your husband," said Alice with a short laugh. "I was fortunate that he's excellent at planning and knows soloists and appropriate hymns and verses. It makes putting a service together so much easier."

The limousine from the funeral home was waiting to take Alice back so she thanked them both and took her leave.

The next day started off very quietly. Beatrice took a walk on a mountain trail with Noo-noo and Wyatt early in the morning. Piper had told Meadow and Beatrice that library story time was at ten and so Meadow had picked her up and they met Piper and Will at the library. The library was one of Beatrice's favorite places anyway—she loved reading the books and magazines in the periodicals section in front of the big gas fireplace. There were big comfy chairs and tables scattered between them where you could put your stack of books.

This time they were in the community room which fit many purposes for the library. The librarian in charge of the "Mother Goose Storytime" had set up a bubble machine as a sort of ice-breaker for the little guys and they watched as the children came in and immediately started crowing with laugher at the bubbles floating around them and reaching up with their chubby hands to swat at them. The librarian had come into the room earlier to decorate it with stuffed animals and set up board books around the room. It all looked fun, cheerful, and welcoming to the little patrons.

"They're so adorable!" said Meadow as she beamed at the kids.

Piper said, "You'd think they'd never be able to settle back down again after this, but the librarian somehow gets them to do it. It must be her superpower."

Sure enough, when the clock struck ten, the librarian blew a party horn and the children watched her in fascination. They all plopped down in a somewhat uneven circle to see what the librarian would do next.

Next happened to be a couple of quieting-down songs to start out the story time and then a wonderful rendition of Sandra Boyton's *Moo, Baa, La La La!* that had all of the children making animal sounds and giving delicious little laughs.

"I want to come to this every week," said Meadow in a stage whisper.

Piper chuckled. "Unfortunately, it's only every two weeks. But you can put it on your schedule."

After *Brown Bear, Brown Bear, What do You See?* by Bill Martin, the librarian worked in a couple of more active songs like "*Head, Shoulders, Knees, and Toes.*" Then there were more bubbles to wrap it all up.

"That was fun," said Beatrice, stretching as she got off the floor.

"I loved every second," said Meadow fervently. "And now we should check out a few books and go to lunch."

"Exactly what I was thinking! As long as it's a toddler-friendly place," said Piper. "I don't want to disturb anyone who's trying to have a relaxing lunch break."

Will found a variety of books and they checked them out at the circulation desk before heading off to find an appropriate place to eat lunch. Will seemed to have a good deal of energy at this point, so it was decided they'd get takeout and eat outside at the park.

Will was happily sitting in his stroller and eating chicken tenders as Meadow, Piper, and Beatrice munched on sandwiches and chatted for a while. The sun was shining brightly on the lake and they could see the ducks on the far side diving for fish. A light breeze wafted around them and they were enjoying the peaceful quiet of the spot. That is, until a siren started blaring.

Meadow frowned. "That sounds like a police siren."

"I have a tough time telling the different sirens apart," said Piper.

The siren sound became closer and Meadow said grimly, "That's *definitely* a police siren. What on earth is going on?"

Beatrice said in a mild voice, "Maybe it's nothing, Meadow. It could be a fender-bender out on the highway. Or someone could have slipped and fallen and needs some help getting back on their feet again."

But then a chorus of sirens—not just police ones—started up. "Something's happened," said Meadow. She took out her phone and tried dialing Ramsay, but he didn't pick up. "No answer."

"Well, if there's an emergency, I can understand why," said Beatrice.

Piper started cleaning up Will's hands with wet wipes and he made some fussy sounds in response. "I should be getting this little guy home, I'm afraid. We're getting dangerously close to naptime."

Meadow took everyone's trash and shoved it into the park's metal can just a few yards away. "Beatrice? Want to follow the sirens?"

Beatrice really wasn't remotely interested in doing that. "We'll likely be very much in the way, Meadow. Besides, won't we seem extremely nosy?"

"Of course not," scoffed Meadow. "I'm the chief of police's wife. You're the minister's wife. We'll be there to *help*."

Beatrice sighed, realizing there was no way to win an argument with Meadow. "If you say so. But let's keep our distance."

Piper and Will set off, waving from their car as Beatrice and Meadow clambered into her minivan.

Meadow set off, windows down to allow her to hear better. "Let's see. They sound like they're heading in that direction. Doesn't it seem that way to you?"

Beatrice was still gloomy about chasing emergency vehicles around town. "Honestly, the sirens seem to be all over the place."

"Yes, and now there are firetrucks and an ambulance, too." Meadow narrowed her eyes and became unusually quiet in order to better hear and follow the sirens.

Eventually, they did find where they were going. It was a cheerful little house with a tidy lawn and lots of flowering bushes.

"Who lives here?" asked Beatrice.

Meadow's eyes were big. "This is where Gail Middleton's mother lives. Oh, goodness. I hope nothing has happened to her mom. Marion is about 90 and hasn't been in the best of health lately."

Beatrice had an uneasy feeling that it might be more likely that Gail herself had an emergency and not her mother. Her suspicions were confirmed at the sight of a frail-looking white-haired woman leaning up against a police car and speaking with an officer. "Isn't that Gail's mom?"

Meadow's eyes grew even larger. "Yes! Oh, no. Does that mean something has happened to *Gail*? But what would Gail have been doing at her mother's house?"

Beatrice bit her lip. She still had no intention of filling Meadow in about the affair. Meadow could be a terrible gossip.

But now, she saw Ralph Middleton spotting her and starting to walk over.

"Look, I'll fill you in later," said Beatrice. "But yes, Gail has been staying with her mom."

"Got it. Well, I suppose her mother has had enough health issues lately to need a couple of extra hands around the house." Meadow peered out the windshield. "Maybe Ralph has some answers."

Ralph's face was ruddy with emotion and his eyes shone as he approached the car. "Beatrice," he said in a choked-up voice. He paused when he saw Meadow with her.

"Ralph, what's wrong?" asked Meadow, looking anxious.

Ralph must have decided that there was no point in trying to cover up past mistakes any longer. "It's Gail. She's dead."

"Oh no," Beatrice murmured. Meadow had been shocked into silence.

Ralph nodded. "I know. I was the one to find her, too. I came over to see how she was doing. I'd been checking in with Marion—that's Gail's mom—every day to find out how Gail was." Meadow was looking confused so Ralph said, "Gail and I have been separated for a little while."

"Oh, no. I'm so sorry," said Meadow. Her brow furrowed with concern.

"This morning, Marion said that Gail was putting her feet up because she had a migraine. I felt terrible because I know how awful Gail's migraines can be. She only gets them when she's really stressed. And I knew that *I'd* been the one who'd caused her all the stress." Ralph swallowed hard, pausing for a couple of moments. "I decided I'd run by and check on her to see how she was doing. He looked down at his hand, which was still clutching something. "I brought over this mask to help her. You put it in the freezer and then wear it after it's nice and cold. It can help with the headache." His voice broke over the last few words.

"And she was . . . *gone*?" asked Meadow.

Ralph took a deep, steadying breath. "Yes. I walked right into the house because Marion has never thought it was necessary to lock her doors here in Dappled Hills. I didn't hear Gail, but figured she might still be lying down. When I walked into the bedroom, though, she was dead. I tried to do CPR on her, but . . ." He shook his head, wordlessly.

"That must have been so frightening," said Beatrice in a low voice.

"I just feel so much guilt about everything," said Ralph. "Maybe Gail wouldn't be dead if she hadn't left home to stay with her mom."

Meadow said, "Was Gail's a *natural* death, Ralph?"

"No way," he said gruffly. "There was a pillow lying over her face. And it's not like *she'd* put it there. No, someone decided to get rid of her."

Meadow's face was stricken.

"Naturally, I'm a suspect," said Ralph. He looked slightly sick, whether with grief or worry. "The spouse is always the primary suspect. And I found her. Ramsay asked me to wait so he could speak with me some more in a few minutes. But I would never lay a finger on Gail."

"Of *course* you wouldn't," said Meadow fiercely from the driver's seat of her car.

"You and I know that, but I'm not sure the police do." Ralph shifted uncomfortably. "In their eyes, I've already hurt Gail. I had an affair, which caused her a good deal of emotional distress."

"Yes, but it's a far cry from having an affair to murdering someone," said Beatrice.

Ralph nodded. "Still, it just makes me sick that I hurt her and caused her pain before the end of her life." He took a deep breath. "Maybe I've got it wrong. Maybe she just passed away in her sleep, pillow or no pillow." His face looked hopeful for a moment at the thought of a peaceful passing for Gail instead of a violent one. "She was pretty young to die like that, but maybe she had some kind of heart event? Like I said, she was under a lot of stress."

Beatrice remembered what Trina had said about how angry Gail had gotten. *Could* her death have somehow been related to her blood pressure? But Gail had been worried about *Ralph's* blood pressure and not her own.

"That's probably what happened," said Meadow stoutly, perking up at the notion that Gail had some sort of natural death. She always hated the idea that Dappled Hills could be any kind of hotbed for murder.

Ralph shook his head. "Either way, it's all just devastating to me. I feel so sad that I've lost Gail and never had the chance to get her to come home to me. I treated her so poorly. All the apologies in the world weren't enough to make up for it. Even worse, when she initially confronted me about it, I was defensive about the affair, and we stayed up all night arguing with each other. I should have begged her forgiveness right away, just as soon as she found out. Instead, I wasted all that time. She was so hurt. And now she's gone."

Someone called Meadow's name and she glanced up. "I'm sorry, Ralph. It looks like Marion wants to speak to me." Fortunately, she looked fully-recovered from her shock as she headed over to talk with Gail's mother.

Ralph looked sad. "Marion probably isn't too sure what to think right now. I doubt she wants to speak with *me*."

"She'll come around," said Beatrice. "She's known you for a long time. She can't think that you'd do something like this to Gail."

Ralph gave a short laugh. "I'm starting to wonder what I'm capable of, myself. I wouldn't have thought I'd have been the kind to cheat on Gail, either."

"I know you said the police were considering you as a suspect. Were you able to give Ramsay an alibi?"

Ralph shook his head. "Not really. That's the thing about being retired—you don't really have an official place to go, do you? This morning I've been at loose ends. I did a little reading and I walked on the treadmill a bit. Then I hopped in the car to bring the migraine mask to Gail. And there's another problem, Beatrice. One that I wanted to tell you about before I talk with the police."

Ralph's features looked even more stressed than before. Beatrice asked, "What is it?"

"I lied to the police before." Ralph looked blankly over to where Ramsay was still being held up speaking to the other officers.

"Lied to them? About what? About Flossie?"

Ralph nodded, releasing a shaky breath. "I just didn't know what to do, Beatrice. I thought they'd arrest me at the time and all I wanted was to get back together with Gail. But I haven't been able to sleep or eat or do anything. This guilt is just weighing down on me."

"Arrest you for what?"

Ralph turned his head to look at Beatrice. "I was the one who found Flossie the day she died. I turned around and left as soon as I discovered her body. I left without calling the police or telling anybody about what I'd found. It was so cowardly of me. I can't even believe I'm talking about myself."

"Okay. So you'd already arrived at Flossie's house for the dinner she was making for you," said Beatrice slowly, trying to piece together what Ralph was telling her.

"That's right. Except I had no intention of sitting down with Flossie and suffering through a meal. I was planning on telling her once and for all that she and I were through. When I got there, I tapped on the door, but she didn't answer. I figured she was on the phone or something and couldn't hear me."

Beatrice said, "And the door was unlocked."

"That's right. Which was very unusual. That's why I'd knocked at her door . . . she kept it locked. She hadn't lived in Dappled Hills very long and wasn't used to the way everybody just left their doors unlocked. Anyway, I walked right in and found her." He gave a small shudder. "I knew right away that she was dead, which is why I didn't call for an ambulance. But I still can't believe that I didn't do the right thing and call the police. Like I said, I feel like I don't even know myself anymore."

Beatrice said, "You must have been completely shocked at what you saw."

"Shocked, yes. Flossie was so full of life. It's tough to picture her gone. And I knew I would be considered a suspect. My gut reaction was to get out of there as quickly as possible. But my gut reaction was wrong; the fact I can't sleep proves that. I need to tell Ramsay the truth. It's not going to make things easy for me, though. I was over there shortly after Flossie was killed. I was heading over to tell her our relationship was done and to stop needling Gail about our affair. I had every reason to be angry with Flossie or end her life because I was furious with her."

"You'd mentioned that Flossie wasn't going to be happy about ending the affair," said Beatrice. "How did you think the evening was going to go?"

"Probably that it would end with Flossie flinging a bunch of food at me," said Ralph wryly. "Flossie wanted to control our relationship and call all the shots. She thought only *she* could decide when it was over. That was the overall theme with everything she did. She shot down Trina's application to be a judge because Flossie wanted to be the only hotshot circuit judge in Dappled Hills."

Beatrice reflected it was also what Flossie had done to Jessica. She'd appointed herself as a gatekeeper for quilting and decided she was the one who could determine who had talent and who didn't. And she also behaved that way in the community, according to Edgenora—Flossie wanted to be the one in control and wanted to force Dora to step back from being in charge of different committees and events.

Ralph said sadly, "I can see it all now, but I couldn't really picture what was happening when I was in the relationship. It's like I couldn't see the forest for the trees. I'm so ashamed of myself now. I think about what you said, Beatrice—that Gail was worried about me being a suspect for Flossie's death. She was still being protective of me and *I* was the one who needed to protect *her*." His voice broke again.

"If Gail's death turns out to be suspicious, do you have any thoughts about who could possibly have harmed her?" asked Beatrice.

Ralph was quiet for a few moments. "Gail was wonderful. That's why I keep going back to the idea that maybe it was some sort of a natural death. Who would have wanted to murder her? She tried her best to get along with everyone and was a friend to so many folks in Dappled Hills. I guess Flossie might have been someone with a motive if she wanted to have me solely to herself. But Flossie died before Gail did. And if anyone thinks that *I* did it, they couldn't be more wrong. All I wanted to do was admit to Gail how much I'd screwed up, ask for forgiveness, and never stray again. I'd have counted my lucky stars every day that she'd taken me back."

He looked absolutely exhausted and miserable. Even more so when Ramsay was finally approaching him with a serious expression on his face. Beatrice said, "Let me know what Wyatt and I can do, Ralph."

He gave her a grateful look. "Thank you. You've done a lot just listening to me as I try to sort all this out. I definitely want to speak with Wyatt soon . . . not only to help me sort out all the feelings I have, but to figure out a service worthy of Gail." His voice cracked once more and he gazed at Meadow and Marion. "I'm not sure my mother-in-law is going to want me to help plan the funeral or not, but I'll make the offer."

Ramsay solemnly greeted Beatrice and she quickly said, "I should gather Meadow and head on."

Ramsay gave her a look that said it might take a lot to pull Meadow away from the scene, but he nodded and he and Ralph walked away from Meadow's car.

Chapter Twelve

FORTUNATELY, MEADOW'S conversation with Marion appeared to have wrapped up and she was already heading back to join Beatrice. She looked around for Ralph and sighed. "Ramsay has him now. I was hoping to talk to Ralph a little."

"Let's head back home," said Beatrice. Meadow still looked a little mulish, so she added, "It's been a while since I've been back and I'm sure Noo-noo would like to go out. Boris probably would, too."

This was the right tactic for Meadow and she immediately hopped into the car. "You're right. And Boris had a lot of water after breakfast today." After she started out driving, she said, "What did you and Ralph talk about?"

"It was mostly Ralph talking about how devastated he was," said Beatrice.

Meadow said, "I'm actually really shocked that Ralph had an affair. He and Gail have always seemed like the perfect couple. Why, they even had a vow renewal ceremony not too long ago! Their grown children were all in town for it and I remember it was a big deal. That's just so *sad*."

"Perhaps we should keep that information under our hats," said Beatrice in a firm voice. "Just to avoid giving Ralph any additional pain."

"Of *course* I'll keep it quiet. Poor Ralph. He's got to be feeling so terribly guilty right now. But you know? I have a feeling that most of the blame for that affair lies with Flossie. I usually don't like to speak ill of the dead, naturally."

Beatrice had seen no evidence of this.

"Flossie, however, is different. Think about all the absolutely rotten things she did in the weeks leading up to her death. No wonder she was murdered!"

Beatrice hid a smile. Meadow was making it sound as if Flossie was some sort of monster instead of simply a deeply flawed person. They were all flawed, to varying degrees.

Meadow was still stewing on Flossie the Horrible as she drove up to Beatrice's cottage. Sure enough, a pair of big ears were visible in the picture window at the front as Noo-noo heard their arrival.

Meadow had really gotten herself worked up this time. Beatrice said, "Now, Meadow. What's done is done. The good thing is that we have Ramsay on the case, figuring out what's happened. He'll make sure there's justice for Gail."

"With your help," said Meadow. "I'm never completely sure that Ramsay's attention is solely focused on his cases. He's always still messing about with his poetry and short stories."

"He always does an excellent job with his police work. Why don't you go home, take Boris out, then put your feet up and look at all the pictures you took from story time today?"

This idea appealed to Meadow and her face softened in a smile. "I did take a lot of pictures. I'll look through them and send you the best ones."

This usually entailed Meadow sending over photos that didn't have her finger obscuring part of the lens. Beatrice nodded encouragingly. "You do that. I'll see you later."

"Okay. I'll let you know if I hear anything from Ramsay." With that, Meadow headed off toward home.

Noo-noo was delighted to see Beatrice and, excuse or not, she was happy to go for a short walk with her as Beatrice collected her thoughts. Could Ralph have had anything to do with Gail's death? It seemed hard to imagine. Ralph could have asked Gail to take him back and then been rejected though and killed her in a rage. That scenario was unlikely, however, considering Gail was apparently smothered in her sleep as she was trying to get over the migraine.

Her phone rang and she fumbled with the leash while she pulled it out of her pocket. It was Posy.

Posy's sweet voice said, "Hi Beatrice! I was trying to think of ways to encourage Jessica with her quilting and I asked her to hold a workshop for us on experimental quilting techniques."

"That's a great idea," said Beatrice. "That should really help her boost her confidence. Did she agree to host one?"

"She was a bit uncertain about it at first, but I told her that none of us were really doing much modern quilting or using experimental techniques and would be interested in finding out more. That she'd be doing us a favor. Then she agreed." Posy sounded pleased.

"Smart approach. When is it going to be?"

Posy chuckled. "Jessica said she wanted to have it soon so she wouldn't lose her nerve. She's giving it in a few days. I'll have to put some signs up at the Patchwork Cottage and maybe something on the shop's social media, too. And make a few phone calls."

"Hopefully there will be a good turnout. I think most of us would like to find out more about experimental techniques, even if we're not interested in trying them, ourselves."

"Fingers crossed!" said Posy.

"Speaking of quilting, how's the group project going so far?" asked Beatrice. "Do we know who has the round robin quilt first? I know the Village Quilters are starting it out before it goes to the Cut-Ups."

Posy chuckled. "I have the quilt first, actually. I figured it might end up being a problem if I didn't because quilters tend to come into the shop and purchase fabric and talk about their project with me. Then I'd end up knowing what other people were doing and I might subconsciously try to match it or coordinate with it."

"Which would entirely defeat the purpose," said Beatrice with a nod. "Smart of you. I didn't even think about that." Beatrice paused. "Not to bring up something a lot darker, but have you heard about Gail?"

Posy paused too, then sounded confused. "Gail? Only what we were talking about—you know. Ralph's affair."

"I'm afraid Gail died this morning," Beatrice said slowly.

"No!" said Posy. "Oh, poor Gail! What happened?"

"We don't really know a lot of details, but it sounds like it might have been under suspicious circumstances."

"Oh, I'm so sorry. Poor Ralph. I know he messed up, but I think he was planning on trying to win Gail back."

Beatrice said, "I think so, too. I'm sorry to break the bad news to you, but thought you'd want to know. Meadow and I were out this afternoon and found out."

"Thanks for letting me know. Do you think it's all right to go ahead with the quilting workshop?" asked Posy worriedly. "I wouldn't want to do anything that might seem disrespectful to Gail's memory."

"I have the feeling that Gail would *want* us to go ahead with the workshop. And it will be nice to have something fun and positive to focus on after the past week."

Posy sounded a bit more cheerful. "That's very true. Thank you, Beatrice. Cork and I will bring some food over to Ralph's house. You and Wyatt take care."

The next couple of days passed quietly. Wyatt preached an excellent sermon. Beatrice cooked vegetables she'd picked up at a roadside stand. Noo-noo had several long walks. Beatrice enjoyed the quieter pace after the upsetting week and spent some time in the hammock reading her book.

Posy had done a good job promoting Jessica's quilting workshop and when Beatrice entered the Patchwork Cottage, she saw lots of quilters there from both guilds. Jessica herself looked a little anxious but smiled and waved to Beatrice when she came in. Everyone had been instructed to bring some food to share and there was a long table fairly groaning with food in the back room. Posy had helped Jessica set up a variety of quilts around the room and Beatrice spent a few minutes taking a look at them. Jessica *did* have talent. It was fun to look at quilts that weren't symmetrical or were minimalist or that had different arrangements of the quilt blocks.

Beatrice filled a plate with different foods. She was trying to be good and eat healthier but decided to take a break from healthy eating when she spotted a baked Vidalia onion dip and crackers. As she suspected, the dip was delicious . . . and filled with a creamy cheese sauce. She took a seat at one of the long tables and glanced around the room. She noted Trina was there with most of the other Cut-Ups. And Alice was there, too, looking rather uncomfortable near the back of the room. Although Alice wasn't a member of any guilds and didn't participate in the quilt shows, she'd always been a casual quilter. Beatrice waved to her and she brightened and came over.

"May I sit next to you?" she asked.

"Absolutely," said Beatrice, sliding the seat out a little. "Don't you want to get some food first, though? I can highly recommend the baked onion dip."

"I'm not too hungry right now, unfortunately. Everything does look really good." She lowered her voice a little, although Beatrice doubted anyone could hear anything over the chatter of voices in the room. "I just wanted to show a little support for Jessica. I still feel awful about how Flossie treated her. I hope my presence here won't be upsetting to Jessica at all. Do you think it will?"

Beatrice shook her head firmly. "No way. I'm sure she really appreciates your being here."

"Well, rightly or wrongly, I still feel terrible about all the trouble Flossie caused in the quilting community. I keep thinking I need to make reparations to everyone."

"You shouldn't worry about that at all, Alice. You're not your sister and no one is going to confuse the two of you," said Beatrice. "You've been here for absolute ages."

Alice gave her a grateful smile as Posy called the workshop to order.

Posy said, "We're in for a real treat today. We have Jessica Brennan here to show us something that may be a little different for some of us—some non-traditional quilts. What I like so much about some of the more modern quilts is how they can expand our view of what quilting can be. We don't have to keep to a particular design or stay within certain parameters. To me, Jessica's quilts are absolutely joyful and full of possibility. To tell you more about them, here she is."

Posy quickly sat back down and the quilters applauded as Jessica walked to the front of the room, looking a bit flushed. Her voice was breathless as she thanked them for being there that day and for Posy's introduction. Then she said in a rush, "Sorry. I'm not used to public speaking."

Miss Sissy, who Beatrice had noted had eaten several plates worth of food, barked, "You're doing fine!"

Everyone chuckled and Jessica relaxed a little. "Thank you, Miss Sissy." She held up a couple of notecards with hands that shook just a bit. "Let's see. I made some notes about where to start." She shuffled quickly through the cards, frowning.

Posy called out in her soft voice, "Maybe you could tell us how you got started with quilting and why you decided on modern quilts."

Jessica looked relieved and started telling the story, getting more natural and relaxed as she went. A few hands went up as she spoke. Beatrice had thought questions should be reserved for the end of the talk, but the questions seemed to make Jessica calmer and more focused. "I think I was really drawn to some of the bold colors and prints. Also, maybe, the idea of breaking the more conventional quilting rules appealed to me." She answered questions about negative space in quilts and using off-center designs. Then Jessica talked about using different stitches for different segments of a project and using stitches to add interest to a quilt by implementing spiral stitching or parallel lines inside a segment. She touched on how she liked creating visual illusions by mixing different shapes together in different sizes, which gave the quilts a sense of movement.

When Jessica finished, there was a round of enthusiastic applause, with Miss Sissy leading the pack. Jessica blushed again, but looked pleased. Beatrice was glad to see quilters lining up to speak with Jessica afterward and even Savannah, a traditional quilter if ever there was one, looked interested in seeing her quilts up-close. As everyone clustered around Jessica, she started to look more sure of herself, more confident. Posy had a pleased smile and walked over to Beatrice.

"I think that went well, don't you?" asked Posy.

"Absolutely. And not only did it work out well for Jessica, we all learned a lot. Honestly, I didn't know much about nontraditional quilts at all. When I worked at the craft museum, I usually handled older, more-traditional pieces." Beatrice glanced around the room. "By the way, I thought I'd stay and give you a hand cleaning up. You had quite a crowd here today."

"Would you? That would be great. Yes, there were more quilters than I hoped might come. I'm so happy that they spread the word."

They chatted for a few minutes while Jessica continued answering questions and talking about the quilts she'd brought in. Eventually, the quilters either headed back out to their cars or walked away to purchase some fabric or other supplies while they were there. Posy hurried off to man the cash register and Beatrice started picking up trash and putting it in the cans.

Soon, just Jessica and Beatrice were left. Jessica started helping Beatrice fold chairs and set them back against the wall.

"That went really well," said Beatrice. "You're quite a natural speaker."

"Do you think so?" asked Jessica shyly. "I was so nervous. I'd practiced with my notecards, but I guess I got everything out of order when I was practicing. It took me a few minutes to hit my stride."

"I think you can just skip the notecards next time, or maybe just have a few bullet points on a single card that help you if you lose track. I liked the way you just started speaking from the heart about how you got into quilting and modern quilting in particular."

Jessica smiled at her. "Thanks so much for being so supportive. I have a habit of always thinking I can do things better than I've done them. I was thinking that I should have had a PowerPoint presentation or brought in some more visual aids or my favorite quilting books or something."

"It was perfect. Instead of thinking how you could have made it better, focus on what you'll do to build on your workshop the next time you do it. All I know is that it provided a wonderful break for me."

Jessica gave her a sidelong look as she threw away a couple of paper plates. "I'm sure you need one, Beatrice. I heard that you and Meadow were on the scene at Gail's house right after she passed. That must have been awful."

"Far worse for poor Ralph," said Beatrice somberly. "I feel terrible for him."

Jessica nodded and said slowly, "I didn't know anything about it for a little while. In fact, I happened on all of the emergency vehicles because I'd gone over to Gail's mom's house around lunch that day to bring her some of my tomatoes. The police stopped me right away, of course, and asked me a bunch of questions." She shrugged. "I told them what I knew, which was nothing."

"That must have been quite a shock to you, coming up on the scene that way."

Jessica said, "Yes. Of course, I knew Gail was living with her mom and I'd heard why. Flossie had mentioned it just right out in the open to me. I couldn't believe she said anything about her affair with Ralph, especially considering Gail and Ralph were still married. She didn't even act like she was ashamed of herself."

Beatrice had the feeling that this was another part of Flossie's plan to break up Gail's and Ralph's marriage. It would be easier if Gail was so humiliated by the entire town knowing about the affair. She might not have wanted to look like the woman who takes back her cheating husband. Gail might, instead, have divorced Ralph and then Flossie could have him as her own.

Jessica took a deep breath. "It felt like the police were asking me a lot of really pointed questions. I'm so worried they think I had something to do with Gail's death. And you know I would *never* do anything to harm Gail. I thought the world of her."

"Did you have a good alibi for the police?" asked Beatrice.

"No, I sure didn't. I was still in bed. No one else was in the house, so I couldn't exactly prove it."

Beatrice asked, "In bed? Weren't you feeling well?" She knew Gail had been in bed, but it had been a migraine that had put her there.

"I wasn't feeling well at all. But it's been like that for days now. I think depression has been fueling it." She gave Beatrice a reassuring smile. "I'm better now, though."

"I'm glad to hear it. It sounds like you've really been through a rough patch."

Jessica said, "Quilting just means so much to me and I felt lost without it."

"You should *definitely* continue quilting. You have a lot of talent and it would be criminal if you didn't continue. I've been looking at the quilts you brought in today and think they're really extraordinary. They're not only good from a visual interest standpoint, but they're also technically very accurate in terms of just basic piecing accuracy and construction."

Jessica flushed happily. "Thanks. You're making me feel a lot better about my work, Beatrice. And I agree with you about continuing in the craft. I've been talking with my doctor and she thinks quilting helps give my life balance. She also suggested doing some jogging to help me with my stress. Once I go home, I'm going to change into workout clothes and do that. And, of course, my friends here have been so great. Posy really helped me get my mojo back by encouraging me and then signing me up for the workshop. Miss Sissy has been wonderful, too."

"Has she?" asked Beatrice. Sometimes Miss Sissy could be helpful, but sometimes it was hard to picture her that way. As was currently the case for Beatrice.

"Yes! She seems really gruff and brusque, but she has such amazing skills. Of course I told you about how I went to her house to see her quilts and to share some of mine. I was shocked that she's excited about seeing different things done with quilting, too—who'd have thought? Plus, she's been really inspiring to me because she works through any arthritis pain she has. Her hands are so gnarled, but she pushes through and still comes up with this beautiful art. She's motivating me to do the same thing. Carl says he can really see a change in my attitude towards life."

"I'm so glad, Jessica. That's wonderful to hear."

Jessica paused and then said, "But going back to what the police think. I know I didn't have any real alibi because I was still in bed. But surely they know that I wouldn't do anything to Gail. She was a friend of mine. I felt terrible for her, actually. After Flossie told me about her affair with Ralph, I could see that Gail knew about it. Of course I didn't tell her that I knew because I just thought that would be so humiliating for her. But I could tell Gail knew about the affair. I bet Flossie told her about it the way she told me."

Jessica continued, "I think that's why I felt such a connection to Gail the last few days. She'd been hurt by Flossie just like I had. And it's hard to reconcile those angry feelings for Flossie with Flossie's death. I feel guilty most of the time."

"Do you have any ideas about who could have harmed Gail?" asked Beatrice softly.

Jessica shrugged. "Not really. At least, not anything definite. But I can't help but wonder if Ralph could possibly be responsible. The spouse is usually the main suspect, right? Ramsay must be investigating that possibility." She gave a short laugh. "Maybe I'm just hoping someone is a bigger suspect than *I* am. But it's a possibility, you know. Maybe Ralph was keeping an eye on the house, watched Gail's mom leave, then slipped in to get rid of Gail."

"But why? Ralph wronged Gail, not the other way around."

Jessica shrugged again, now looking more despondent. "That's what doesn't really make sense. Maybe he was trying to get Gail to come back to him and got angry when she wouldn't. Or maybe Ralph thought Gail knew he'd killed Flossie and he wanted to make sure she didn't tell anyone what she knew. At any rate, surely Ralph must have had a better motive to kill *Flossie* than I did. I know I had a big blow-up with Flossie. It was just my surprise when Flossie totally ravaged my work. I was expecting to hear compliments from her or some encouraging words and it came as a total shock when she was so down on my quilts. But I hadn't been *mad*. I was just upset and burst into tears."

"A totally normal reaction," murmured Beatrice.

"Flossie, on the other hand, *was* angry. She said I needed to learn how to keep it together and my emotions in check if I ever thought I was going to make it to the big regional quilt shows. Flossie said that no one was going to care about my delicate feelings when my quilts were being judged. That's really just bunk, though. Everyone I've met has given me nothing but support and encouragement, even when they were giving me ideas for ways to improve. Other quilters *want* me to do well. They're pulling for me and they're excited to see something a little different at the shows. Now I'm able to put Flossie's words into perspective. At the time, though, I totally overreacted."

"Which is understandable. And now, Jessica, I think you deserve to go home and get ready for your jog before you're just completely exhausted. You did a fantastic job and there's no need to spend your remaining energy cleaning up when you could do some focused exercising."

Jessica grinned at her. "Words from the wise. You're so right. Thanks, Beatrice."

After Jessica collected her quilts and notecards and left, Posy came back in the room after finishing with the swarm of quilters at the cash register. Beatrice was just finishing wiping down the tables and chairs.

"Goodness! You're already finished," said Posy, looking pink in the face. "I didn't mean for you to do all the work."

"Jessica helped me put chairs away for a while before I dismissed her," said Beatrice with a chuckle. "It was no trouble at all. The workshop was marvelous, and you were smart to come up with it. I should head on back myself now, though."

Posy gave her a warm hug and thanked her again and Beatrice left for the cottage, where cuddles with Noo-noo awaited her.

Chapter Thirteen

THE NEXT AFTERNOON, Piper called to ask if Beatrice could watch Will for her. Since Beatrice took advantage of every single opportunity she could to spend time with her grandson, she happily accepted. Will gave her a happy smile when he toddled in, showing off his collection of baby teeth. Beatrice hugged him and said, "I set out toys from the toy chest for you."

Will rushed off to play with Noo-noo practically skipping along beside him. The little dog loved Will and always sat as close as possible to him.

"How did Jessica's workshop go yesterday?" asked Piper.

Beatrice filled her in and Piper smiled. "Oh, good. I felt bad that I couldn't make it and was hoping there was a good turnout. That makes me feel better about not being there."

They chatted for a couple more minutes before Piper left for her doctor appointment and a few other errands. Beatrice settled in to play with Will for a little while until there was a knock at the door. Beatrice frowned, wondering if Piper had forgotten something.

When she opened the door, however, it was Miss Sissy standing there. The old woman seemed to have a gift for knowing when the baby was at Beatrice's house. Either that, or she camped out across the street with a pair of binoculars.

"Hi, Miss Sissy," said Beatrice with a distinct lack of enthusiasm. "How are you today?"

Miss Sissy grunted and swept past Beatrice into the cottage. Will grinned at the old woman as she walked up and offered her a toy truck to play with. Miss Sissy's eyes twinkled at him—an experience that Beatrice had observed only happened with Will. They started to play and Beatrice wryly realized she might as well read her book nearby—Miss Sissy was not a fan of having others interrupt her playtime.

After twenty minutes or so, Miss Sissy reached into the large, quilted tote bag she'd brought with her and pulled out a couple of sandwich bags with some sort of cracker-like snack in them.

Beatrice frowned. "I'd better check with Piper first. She has a list of approved foods for Will."

Miss Sissy glowered at her. "Already did!" she hissed at Beatrice.

It was very organized of Miss Sissy to check with Piper first. And organization was not ordinarily one of Miss Sissy's traits.

Beatrice realized Miss Sissy was in a huff, so she held out an olive branch. "May I try your snack?" she asked penitently.

Miss Sissy grudgingly handed her one of the snack bags. As Beatrice ate, she asked, "Didn't you think Jessica's workshop went well?"

Now the old woman broke into a smile. "Yes! Smart girl."

Beatrice was relieved to see Miss Sissy in a better mood. She rambled on about Jessica's talents for a moment as Miss Sissy nodded enthusiastically at Beatrice's praise.

Then the old woman abruptly changed topics. Beatrice should have been used to her non-sequiturs, but they always managed to startle her. "Gail died."

"Yes. Yes, she did," agreed Beatrice, not sure where this was going. Will, oblivious, made truck noises and continued playing.

Miss Sissy sniffed. "Hung out with Dora."

This was news to Beatrice. Dora and *Flossie* had "hung out." Dora and Flossie had *argued*. But, although Gail was a member of the Cut-Ups along with Flossie and Dora, Beatrice had never really seen Gail and Dora together in any form or fashion.

"Did she?" There must have been an element of doubt in Beatrice's voice because the old woman's eyes narrowed menacingly.

"She did!"

Beatrice nodded in an encouraging way, hoping to get Miss Sissy back on more even keeling. "That's good. I think Gail has needed a friend recently."

Miss Sissy gave Beatrice a disdainful look and didn't dignify her response with an answer, instead picking up a toy truck and commencing to play with Will again.

The phone rang and Beatrice picked up.

A wavering female voice hesitated and then asked, "Is Wyatt there?"

"No, I'm sorry, he's not. I believe he's visiting the nursing homes today. This is Beatrice . . . may I take a message for him? Or may I help?"

There was a pause and then the woman said, "Hi, Beatrice. It's Marion. Gail's mom."

"Marion. Oh, I'm so sorry about Gail."

Marion gave a shaky sigh on the other side. "Thank you, dear, I feel like I should be handling this better. At my age, I've seen a lot of loss. But it's just too hard to lose a child."

"Of course it is. I'm sorry I can't connect you with Wyatt right now. He did get in touch with you earlier, I hope?" Beatrice frowned, trying to remember what Wyatt had been talking about the past day. It seemed like a blur of hospital visits and planning for a wedding, but Beatrice was sure he'd said he'd gone over to see Marion.

"He did. Wyatt is so lovely and kind, Beatrice. He helped a lot with planning a service for Gail." Marion's voice broke a little during the last few words."

"Good. I'm glad to hear that. Do you need anything from the church at all? I hope the bereavement group has been by."

Marion said, "Oh, I have so much food, Beatrice. My fridge and freezer are bursting with it. I don't think I'll ever have to cook again."

Beatrice gave a small smile. The bereavement committee was quite good at killing with kindness. They'd show up every day with casseroles, breads, and lunch fixings until they were basically called off. "That's great to hear that they've left you in good shape."

Marion said, "I know Wyatt is so busy. I really hate to bother him."

"Oh, Wyatt doesn't look at it as a bother at all! He wants to help."

"Just the same, Beatrice, I feel bad diverting him from all the other good works he's doing. I was mainly calling because I need to talk. I have so many things running through my head right now and I thought it might help me to talk them out."

Beatrice glanced across the room to where Miss Sissy and Will had pulled books off the coffee table and made tunnels for the toy trucks to be pushed through. "Would it help at all if you speak with me? I can promise, confidentiality, of course. I'm not as helpful as Wyatt, but I've been told I'm decent at listening. I'd come over to your house but unfortunately, I have my grandbaby here with me now." And Miss Sissy, who made life just about as complicated.

Marion sounded relieved. "You wouldn't mind a little chat then? I hate taking you away from your grandson."

"He's occupied with toy trucks right now so it's no trouble at all."

Marion took a deep breath and launched right in, perhaps concerned that she wouldn't be able to get a full conversation in with a baby nearby.

"I just have so many things on my mind now. It's horrible, Beatrice. Having this happen right in my own home is incredibly upsetting and is really messing up my head. I feel like everyone is a potential enemy. I don't know who to trust." There was a pause and then Marion said, "I know that sounds awful, but it's how I feel. It's just that I'm living in a house that always felt safe. I never even locked the doors in all the years I've lived here. Then my daughter was murdered in that house, most likely by someone I know well and trusted."

"That must be a horrible feeling," said Beatrice slowly.

"It is. I've started locking the doors all the time, even when I'm at home. It makes me feel like a prisoner. And every time my doorbell rings or someone knocks on my door, I jump half a mile. I'm so cautious. I even picked up pepper spray at the hardware store and keep it on the table next to my front door."

"I think, under the circumstances, that's a smart thing to do."

Marion said, "I've been thinking about moving. I can hardly believe I'm thinking that way. I've lived in this house for fifty years and thought I'd live here the rest of my days. And now, I don't feel safe here. Every single time I pass by my guest room, I think about Gail and how awful her last few moments must have been."

Beatrice said, "I can understand why you'd feel that way, Marion. I hate that this has happened to you and to Gail."

"And that's not all. I can't help but wonder if just about everybody is a potential suspect. There's someone out there who Gail and I thought was a friend who turned out to be dangerous. It's a terrible way to live." She hesitated and then said, "Although everyone has been so helpful and kind—even before Gail died. Folks have come over and been very supportive. Most of the quilting guild has been in and out of my door. And not just the Cut-Ups—the Village Quilters, too."

Beatrice said, "It's one of those situations where we all want to help, but there's not much we can do."

"That's just it. I can tell they are just dying to do something to help me out, but there's nothing to sort out except my own grief." She paused again. "I hate to say this, Beatrice, but there's something I've been thinking a lot about. I'm not sure if I should say anything to Ramsay or not."

This sounded just like Posy. And Beatrice's advice was the same. "If it's anything that might pertain to Gail's death, I think Ramsay would want to know about it."

"I know. I'm just so conflicted. You see, I don't really know anything. I'm just passing on hearsay. And the person it involves might get into trouble and he might not have done anything at all."

Beatrice realized Marion must be talking about Ralph. "Still, I think it's important to let Ramsay sort out what's important information and what's not."

Marion said, "That's why it's nice speaking with you, Beatrice. You're always so very sensible. The thing is, Gail was convinced that Ralph was involved in Flossie's death."

"Was she?"

Marion added sadly, "I suppose you know about Ralph's infidelity. It just about broke Gail's heart. I hate that my girl had to go through that right before she died."

"Gail did fill me in. I was sorry to hear about it."

Marion said, "Yes. Gail decided that Ralph must have been going through some sort of midlife crisis. I did think he was a bit long in the tooth for that sort of nonsense, but I didn't want to upset Gail more than she already was. Anyway, Ralph was frantic to get Gail back. Gail moved right into my house of course, to lick her wounds for a while. Ralph came over every single day, pleading with her to speak with him and to get back together with him."

"Would Gail see him?" Beatrice looked back over at Miss Sissy and Will. They were now reading a book together. Actually, it looked as if Will was trying to tell the story to the old woman and making it up as he went along.

Marion said, "Sometimes Gail would talk to him and sometimes she wouldn't. A few times Gail had me send him away. Ralph would have such a hangdog expression that I felt bad for him. It's hard to imagine *me* feeling sorry for *him* after he'd upset Gail so much, but that's just how I felt. Gail said Ralph told her that he was going to break it off with Flossie right away—that he'd made a terrible mistake and could see the error of his ways."

Beatrice said, "So Gail thought Ralph went over to speak with Flossie and things got out of control?"

Marion's voice sounded relieved that Beatrice had guessed correctly. "That's exactly it. She thought that maybe Flossie flew into a rage and Ralph was protecting himself. Or that something happened accidentally and then Ralph fled. It makes me wonder . . . what if Gail confronted Ralph with her suspicions?"

"You think Ralph made one of his regular visits to your house and Gail got him to confess to her?"

"Maybe," said Marion. "Maybe Gail told him she thought he did it and he was startled into confessing. Then he came back the other day, worried she was going to tell the police, and murdered her." Her voice broke over the last few words.

Beatrice said slowly, "Well, that certainly sounds plausible. Is that what you think happened?"

"I don't know. I hate to think so. Ralph and Gail always seemed so very happy together. I can't picture him ending her life like that. Honestly, I was more concerned that Ralph might harm *himself* since that's the sort of state he was in. Besides, there were others who might have done it."

"Are there?" asked Beatrice.

Marion dithered a little on the phone and then said in a rush, "Again, I don't want to cast suspicion on people who might be completely innocent. I don't know *anything*."

"I'll be sure to keep this as quiet as I can."

Marion took a deep breath and continued, "Alice. Alice was over at my house to see Gail after Flossie died. She wanted, I think, to apologize on behalf of her sister. But it didn't go especially well."

"Oh?"

"No. I could tell Alice felt terrible about Flossie's affair with Ralph. She was trying to mend bridges—not that Alice had directly done anything at all to Gail. Unfortunately, Gail wasn't in the right frame of mind for a visit from Alice. She was pretty sharp with her." Beatrice heard Marion sigh over the line. "I told Gail afterward that Alice didn't deserve that harshness when she was trying to make amends on her sister's behalf. Alice just looked so dejected. Gail ended up feeling bad about it and tried to apologize afterward for being sharp, but Alice hung up the phone when she realized it was Gail. I guess she thought Gail was going to have another rant."

Beatrice said, "So you think Alice might have been upset or hurt by Gail's reaction? Enough to harm her?"

"It sounds so silly when you put it that way. I don't know—like I said, I'm really just grasping at straws."

Beatrice said gently, "I think you're trying to figure out what happened to your daughter and maybe find a little closure at the same time. Please do tell Ramsay what you've seen and heard. It might help and it certainly won't do any harm."

"Thank you, Beatrice," said Marion in a quiet voice. "You've been a real dear."

Marion hung up and Beatrice looked back over at Miss Sissy and Will. Reading stories together had apparently made Miss Sissy drop off into a nap. Will was happily back playing with his trucks while the old woman snored on the sofa.

A sudden wild banging and whining at Beatrice's front door startled all of them. Noo-noo started barking furiously as Will looked on in wonder as the little dog transformed into a watchdog.

Chapter Fourteen

BEATRICE PEERED CAUTIOUSLY out the front window, expecting to see some sort of dangerous person on her doorstep. Instead, she saw the happy and slightly dim features of Boris-the-dog.

"Oh, for heaven's sake," muttered Beatrice as she opened the door.

Boris bounded in, no longer the good boy who'd been so docile during the guild meeting. Clearly tired of behaving like a model citizen, he'd escaped from Meadow and ended up in familiar territory at Beatrice's house.

Noo-noo stopped barking and the two dogs sniffed a hello to each other.

Miss Sissy looked disdainfully at Boris from across the room. Although she was very much an animal lover, those feelings didn't really extend to Boris, who she viewed as entirely too unpredictable.

"Where did I put that extra leash?" muttered Beatrice to herself, looking around the room.

Will stood up and toddled over to see Boris as Beatrice was still wracking her brain over the leash. She was about to scoop

Will up when Boris plopped down on the floor, rolled on his back, and suddenly became as meek and gentle as a lamb. Beatrice had witnessed how sweet the big dog was with Will, but had figured Boris was too wound up to properly behave this time. Miss Sissy protectively sat next to Will as he rubbed Boris's tummy as gently as he could.

Beatrice found the leash and put it on Boris, just in case.

Then the phone rang again, earning a glare from Miss Sissy at the extra interruption.

Beatrice answered, wondering if Marion had forgotten to mention something.

But it was Meadow. "Hi, Beatrice. Is Boris paying you a visit?" Meadow sounded a bit harried.

"Hi, Meadow. Yes, Boris decided to come over and say hi," said Beatrice drolly. "Would you like to come collect him?"

"Umm, well, ordinarily I would. But let me ask you another question. Is Miss Sissy over there by any chance?"

"Yes, she's over here playing with Will. Is anything wrong?"

Something apparently *was* very wrong because Miss Sissy's eyes got really large and she started vehemently shaking her head.

Meadow said, "Well, thank heavens. I was wondering where she was. Miss Sissy has a dental appointment and I'm supposed to drive her there. I didn't realize the responsibility would include tracking her down first. I've been calling all over town."

Miss Sissy was now quietly trying to slip out Beatrice's door.

"Meadow is running by to take you to the dentist," said Beatrice sternly.

Miss Sissy winced and then looked sullen.

"Can you keep her there?" asked Meadow.

"I can, but you should probably hurry. Don't you have a moment to run Boris by the house before you head downtown?"

"There's just no time. I'm worried they'll cancel her appointment. Do you mind keeping him there?" And she hung up before waiting for an answer.

Meadow was there in just a minute and flew through the door. "Let's head on out, Miss Sissy. We're running late and have to get your teeth taken care of."

Miss Sissy did not look pleased by this prospect.

Boris grinned unrepentantly at his mistress and she sighed as she spotted him.

Then Meadow caught sight of her grandson and catapulted herself across the room for a few seconds of cuddling. Finally, squaring her shoulders, she tore herself away, told Boris to be a good boy, and herded the slouching Miss Sissy out the door for the appointment.

Will paused in his playing, looking fairly astonished at all the rapid comings and goings. Beatrice decided this might be a good time to introduce an entire change of location for them, too. "Would you like to go to the playground?"

Will grinned up at her and it was decided. At first, Beatrice thought she might drive them over, but then figured a walk might do her good. First she pulled down an old blanket for Boris, filled another water bowl, and gave both Boris and Noo-noo snacks. Then she made sure that all food items were completely out of Boris's reach (the dog had a pretty substantial reach). She then bundled Will into the stroller and they headed off toward downtown Dappled Hills.

As always, Will loved to see everything along the way—birds perched in trees and bushes, people working in their yards, and folks going in and out of stores downtown. An airplane buzzed overhead and he craned his neck to track it as it made its way across the sky. One of Beatrice's favorite parts of being a grandmother was to see the world through Will's eyes. It made everything seem fresh and new again.

The park and playground were right in the middle of downtown, which made it a fun location to visit. There were lots of people walking on the trails in the park (one of which connected with a hiking trail that scaled a mountain) and sitting on benches eating ice cream from the downtown ice cream shop. Will took it all in, including the part of the playground which was for older children with plastic rock-climbing walls and big playground equipment. Beatrice, though, steered them toward the little-kid playground with the baby swings, sandbox, and smaller slide and climbing equipment. As they approached, Beatrice spotted Alice Hall sitting on a bench nearby and reading a book—not an unexpected pastime for a librarian.

"Hi," Beatrice called out.

Alice looked up from her book and smiled. "Oh, my goodness, you've got your grandson with you! Hi there, sweetie."

Will beamed up at her and shyly stuck his finger in his mouth.

"We're just heading over to the playground for the little guys," said Beatrice. She paused. "It's good to see you out and about."

Alice nodded. "I decided I couldn't hide from everyone in town anymore. I do still feel bad about Flossie and how much trouble she caused."

"Yes, but as I said before, it's not *you* that caused any trouble. No one is confusing the two of you."

Alice looked a little sad. "I wish I could believe that, Beatrice. I even ran into trouble with Gail, bless her soul."

Beatrice remembered what Marion had told her on the phone about an argument with Gail blowing up at Alice. "Trouble with her?"

"That's right. I'd gone over to check on Gail. I didn't really feel I could apologize to Gail on behalf of Flossie, but I wanted to make sure that *our* friendship was unscathed by Flossie's affair with Ralph. I went over to Marion's house with some bread I'd baked. I chatted with Marion for a few minutes and then she walked out of the room and Gail just lit into me." Alice winced unhappily at the memory.

"About Flossie's affair?"

"Yes. I guess she thought I'd known about it before she had and had conspired with Flossie to conceal it from everyone. But I had no idea." Alice spread her hands wide. "I told her that and Gail just kept on ranting. Marion heard her and came in and Gail burst into tears. I left as soon as I could. She did try calling me back after I got back home, but I didn't pick up because I worried she was going to rant some more. And now . . . well, I can't believe she's gone. I feel so bad that I didn't talk to her on the phone that last time. And now, I'm still just as shocked as I was when I found out she passed. Ramsay's been asking me more questions and once again I have no alibi whatsoever. I'm unbelievably inept at having alibis. I told him I was at home, reading the newspaper, drinking coffee, and eating a pimento cheese sandwich."

Beatrice asked, "How did you find out about Gail?"

"From Ramsay. I was having a quiet day inside and he came by. He was trying to figure out if I knew of any connection between Flossie's death and Gail's."

"Did you?"

Alice shook her head. "Not at all. In fact, I was just so stunned by Gail's death that I'm sure I wasn't helpful at all. The first thing that came to my mind when Ramsay said Gail was dead is that she must have self-harmed. I'd seen firsthand how unstable she seemed—she was so unhappy about the affair. I thought she might have been desperate. But then Ramsay told me it wasn't suicide . . . it was murder. I couldn't seem to wrap my head around it." She looked at Beatrice with her piercing eyes. "Are people saying it was Ralph?"

Beatrice said noncommittally, "I haven't been out much myself, lately. Not to get a sense of what the word around Dappled Hills, is, anyway."

Alice nodded absently. "I wish I could have been a better friend to Gail. Now, when I think back to our last meeting, it makes me so sad. When she was railing at me about Flossie, I feel it was almost a cry for help. I should have just taken her in my arms and let her cry it all out instead of walking away."

Beatrice said, "Hindsight is 20/20. Remember that it was also important for you to protect yourself and your own feelings. You've gone through a terrible time, too—you've lost a sister and you're feeling uncomfortable in a town you've lived for many years. You shouldn't blame yourself for heading home when Gail became so upset."

"Thanks, Beatrice. You're right, as usual. I didn't really think of it from that perspective." Alice sighed. "Now I just want to get my life back on track again. Nothing was the same after Flossie moved to Dappled Hills. It's time to get back into my old routines and pick up with my old friends again."

"That's smart of you," said Beatrice. "I think most of us do better when we have some sort of daily regimen. I need to work on mine."

"I'm exercising again. Not a lot, but taking regular walks and lifting some light hand weights at home. I feel so much better and now I'm *sleeping* so much better. It really helps me reduce my stress levels. It's amazing how much my body has missed the exercise." She lowered her voice as if someone might overhear and said, "I've cut back on drinking, too. I realized I was purchasing wine far too frequently at the grocery store. And I'm trying to make a point of calling folks I haven't been in touch with for a while just to check in."

"And you're going to the park and enjoying a beautiful day," said Beatrice with a smile.

"Exactly. For once, I feel really hopeful. I mean, I still do feel guilty about everything, especially the fact that I'm profiting from Flossie's death. I may give most of it away after I put a bit in for an emergency fund."

Beatrice said, "That sounds like a wonderful tribute to Flossie."

Alice gave a short laugh. "There has to be *something* good to come out of all of this." She paused. "Aside from Ralph, do you know who the police might be considering as a suspect? Besides me, of course."

Beatrice quickly shook her head. "I'm afraid not."

"You haven't noticed police cars outside people's houses or that sort of thing?"

Beatrice shook her head again. "I'm sorry."

Alice nodded and was quiet for a few moments. Then she said, "I did see something recently that made me wonder. I saw Gail speaking with Jessica the day before Gail died. Gail was quite animated. I couldn't help but wonder what all that was about."

Alice gave Beatrice a searching look and Beatrice said, "I haven't heard anything about that. Did Gail seem angry or just upset?"

"It was hard for me to tell. You know, it was probably nothing. The last thing I need is more guilt because I started a rumor."

"I won't say a word," said Beatrice.

Alice colored a little. "Of course you won't. I don't know why I even said that. And what I saw between Gail and Jessica was probably nothing. Gail was probably wound up because she was complaining about Ralph again. I shouldn't be worried about other people—I should be worried about myself, considering I keep having to speak with Ramsay. I know what it all looks like. Flossie and I were publicly at odds sometimes. But what people don't understand is that I loved my sister, regardless of the way she embarrassed me sometimes. And I certainly hope no one would seriously suspect me of killing Gail."

Will gave a happy chuckle as a butterfly landed close by. Alice gazed wistfully at him as if wishing for a return to a similar innocence and simplicity.

"He's been such a patient little guy," said Alice.

Beatrice gave her grandson a proud look. "He takes in everything around him which makes him especially easy to entertain."

"Well, he deserves to play now. Good talking to you, Beatrice."

And she delved back into her book.

Will played enthusiastically on the playground equipment, going down the small plastic slide over and over again and then carefully hurrying up the stairs. Another toddler joined him after a few minutes and he played alongside him in the sandbox until both children started tossing sand around. Beatrice decided the swings were in order and plopped Will into the toddler swing. After a few minutes, she saw he was looking sleepy as he swung and glanced at her watch. Sure enough, it was a bit past his usual naptime.

"We need to head back to the house and check on the puppy dogs," said Beatrice and Will gave her a sleepy smile in response.

Will nodded off a couple of times in the stroller, which meant Beatrice had to wake him up on some pretense or another—pointing out the bright red of a cardinal or the way a small bunny froze as they approached it. She knew if he napped in his stroller that he'd never get a full nap in, which wouldn't be good for Beatrice *or* Piper.

As soon as they got inside and were greeted by Noo-noo and Boris, Beatrice put Will down with his teddy bear in the portable crib she kept in her second bedroom. She sang a lullaby to him in her warbling singing voice and he fell asleep about halfway through it.

She tiptoed out of the room and carefully shut the door behind her when there was a rat-a-tat-tat of a knock on her front door. Boris and Noo-noo started barking and Beatrice grimaced and hurried to open it before they knocked again and woke Will from his nap.

When she opened the door, she saw Meadow standing there, looking around for Will.

"Where's my little guy?" she asked in her usual loud Meadow voice as she reached down to rub Boris. "I hated having to run out of here without really being able to visit with him."

"He's sleeping," said Beatrice in a pointedly hushed voice. "Let's step outside in the backyard. I'll grab the baby monitor."

Meadow glanced regretfully toward the bedroom but nodded and followed Beatrice into the backyard as Noo-noo and Boris joyfully followed.

Chapter Fifteen

THEY SAT AT THE TABLE under the trees and Meadow said sadly, "Pooh. I'm sorry I didn't come earlier." She looked hopeful. "Has he been asleep for a while?"

"No, I just put him down."

Meadow made a face. "Oh well. I'll see him tomorrow. It was just hard to pop in, collect Miss Sissy for her dental appointment, and then run out again without getting a chance to visit with Will."

"How did the dental appointment go?"

Now Meadow made even more of a face.

"Miss Sissy, as we feared, had several cavities. Which is, apparently, why she so dislikes having to go to the dentist. I'm going to let someone else have the task of hauling her over there next time."

Beatrice said, "I could tell she wasn't very enthusiastic about it."

"That's putting it mildly. After we got to the dentist office, I was still collecting my purse and putting my car keys away and she'd sprinted off down the sidewalk! I had to run after her and persuade her to go into the building. I was totally frazzled by the time it was all over. I kept thinking she was going to charge out of her cleaning wearing the cape and tear off down the street."

"I'll drive her to her next appointment," said Beatrice. "It sounds like it's something of a vicious cycle, isn't it? She doesn't *want* to go because she's scared of having cavities that need filling. But she has cavities that need filling because she doesn't go to the dentist."

"Exactly! It's all very exhausting. And this was *after* Boris-the-escape-artist bolted through the front door when I'd stepped out to water my flowers. It's been a very trying day."

And indeed, Meadow did look very tired. She was slumping in her chair and kept casting longing looks at the hammock.

"Do you need to take a nap?" asked Beatrice, her eyes twinkling.

"Don't tempt me! Part of me wants to join Will in the napping room and conk out for a while. But I know if I fall asleep now that I won't be able to get any good sleep tonight." She added, "And of course I came over to see Will, but I'm glad to have the chance to speak with you about everything. The last time I had the opportunity to talk with you we were over at poor Gail's house. What are you thinking about who the likely murderer might be?"

Beatrice opened her mouth and Meadow quickly interjected, "But don't tell me it's Jessica, Trina, or Dora! Or Alice either—she's not in a guild, but she quilts, too."

Naturally, Meadow had wanted her to leave out all the quilters. Beatrice said wryly, "So we're down to Ralph, are we?"

Meadow had the grace to look a bit guilty. "That's horrible, isn't it? But you have to admit that Ralph seems to be the cause of all the trouble."

"I thought you'd decided that *Flossie* was the cause of all the trouble."

Meadow shrugged. "I think she was the instigator, but it's not as if she murdered anyone. The point of this exercise is to figure out who might be Flossie's killer. That way, Ramsay can arrest him or her and we can get on with normal life in Dappled Hills."

"Got it."

Meadow said, "So let's think about Ralph first of all, since we've already brought him up. He kickstarted all of this by having an affair with Flossie. He certainly had the motive for *both* of the murders. And he would have had plenty of opportunity. He really does seem to be our top choice, doesn't he?"

"He does and he doesn't," said Beatrice slowly.

Meadow frowned at her. "What does that mean?"

"I agree that he definitely had a good opportunity to harm both Flossie and Gail. And I agree that he had an excellent motive to kill Flossie."

Meadow snorted. "I'll say! Flossie was actively trying to end his marriage to Gail. He must have been furious with her."

"But the fact is that I have a tough time seeing Ralph murdering Gail. The whole point was that he was trying to get back together with her. Why would he have ended her life? He seems really devastated by the loss, too." She paused. "Alice mentioned to me that maybe Ralph had to murder Gail because she was aware he'd killed Flossie. But I really can't see it."

Meadow gave a gusty sigh. "I guess so. It's a pity because then it means that one of our friends might be responsible for all this. What do you think about Dora?"

Beatrice thought a lot about Dora Tucker. She thought Dora was incredibly self-driven, efficient, and hard-working. But she also thought that Dora liked getting her own way and was inclined not to delegate but to completely take over events and projects in order to run it the way she saw fit. But she wasn't sure she wanted to share these thoughts with Meadow. "What do you think about her?" she instead asked in a carefully diplomatic manner.

"I think she's a real asset to the quilting community, of course! And the church community. And just about any other community she's involved with. But I am a little worried about that argument she had with Flossie before Flossie's death. From what you said, it sounded very heated."

Beatrice said, "Yes, but just about everyone quarreled with Flossie before she died. Jessica being one of them."

Now Meadow looked especially down in the dumps. "I suppose you're right. And Alice was also always at odds with her sister, wasn't she?"

"I think she was mainly just embarrassed and frustrated by Flossie's shenanigans."

Meadow said, "Those two were just nothing at all alike. You have Alice as the responsible sibling who doesn't like to make waves at all and then Flossie, a newcomer to Dappled Hills, blowing up relationships left and right. I think Flossie must have enjoyed it." Boris nudged Meadow's hand and she gave him a loving rub.

"I do think she liked to create drama. Maybe it kept her entertained. She'd had a really busy, active life and then she moved to a small town. Flossie might have been looking for ways to relieve her boredom."

Meadow sighed. "It sort of sounds like Flossie: causing trouble because she had too much energy and not enough to do. And then there's Trina. Yet another quilter. And she had good reason to be unhappy with Flossie since Flossie totally sabotaged her efforts to be a quilt show circuit judge."

"Anyone really could have done it," said Beatrice. "I'm afraid we're just going to have to have more information before everything becomes clear. Ramsay is sure to uncover something."

Meadow didn't look so sure. "He's trying, I will say that for him." Her tone was grudging. "I haven't seen him writing or reading his book lately."

"I hope he's had *some* downtime, at least. He's getting sleep and eating regularly?"

Meadow pursed her lips. "As far as I can tell, he's not doing much of either. He looks absolutely exhausted whenever I do lay eyes on him. And whenever I offer him food, he waves it away. At this rate, I think he might waste away."

Beatrice very much doubted this would happen. Ramsay was quite generously proportioned, due to Meadow's marvelous culinary skills and the fattening Southern meals she preferred cooking.

Meadow sighed again and squinted at her watch. "Suppose I should head on out, since I can't visit with the baby. Maybe I can make an especially alluring supper that will encourage Ramsay to eat."

"What qualifies as alluring?" asked Beatrice curiously.

"Meatloaf, cheesy mashed potatoes, and fried okra." Meadow's answer was prompt, demonstrating her excellent knowledge of Ramsay's tastes after decades of married life. "Which means I should go to the store." She frowned thoughtfully. "Actually, meatloaf might be easy for Miss Sissy to eat, too, after her dental work. I'll make a couple of loaves and take one over to her. It'll be something of a peace offering since she was so furious with me for taking her to the dentist."

After Meadow left with a cheerfully unrepentant Boris in tow, Beatrice decided she needed to settle on a quiet activity inside so she could hear Piper when she returned. She brushed Noo-noo, which wasn't Noo-noo's idea of fun. The little dog was good, though, and silently endured the thorough brushing Beatrice gave her. So much of the corgi's undercoat came off that Beatrice felt she could practically make another dog out of it. After a little while, there was a light tap on the door. Beatrice smiled. It had to be Piper. She was used to keeping sleeping babies asleep.

Piper gave Beatrice a quick hug after she came in. "How did it go?" she asked in a hushed voice. "I'm guessing Will is napping?"

"Sound asleep. But he should be good to wake up whenever you need to leave—he's had a pretty decent nap."

"How about if I visit for a couple of minutes and then wake him up?"

Beatrice nodded, always happy for an opportunity to visit with her daughter. Beatrice took the monitor again and they headed into the backyard. It was, of course, much more of a relaxing visit than the one with Meadow.

"How are things going?" asked Beatrice. She hoped that Piper was feeling less conflicted and guilty over her time away from the baby . . . and her time away from work.

"Better," said Piper with a smile for her mother. "Thanks for talking me off the cliff the other day. It helps to mull things over with someone else."

"How does Ash feel about your schedule?"

Piper gave her a rueful look. "He's mostly just trying to make sure I'm not stressed out. You know the old saying: 'happy wife, happy life.'"

"Sounds like a smart man," said Beatrice. She wasn't surprised that Ash's focus was on Piper and making sure she was content.

"I've kind of made peace with the work side of things. I reminded myself that I'm a part-time worker and there's just no way that my work is done at the end of my day. I don't need to take it home with me and do it; I just start knocking it out the next day when I get there."

Beatrice said, "Sounds like job security to me. You always have work to do when you show up. I'm glad to hear you're not taking it home at night—that's your time with Will and Ash."

"Exactly. And, it looks like, with home improvement projects."

Beatrice raised her eyebrows. "Really?"

"Well, they're more the kind of projects that make themselves known instead of projects we identify and plan for," said Piper wryly.

"Uh-oh. Those are the types of home improvement projects that sound unexpected and expensive."

"Right—some plumbing stuff, some air conditioning work. But the nice thing is that Ash is pretty good at tinkering with most things and his promotion means that we can more easily pay someone to take care of the things he can't." Piper reached out again for Beatrice's hand and said, "Now, Mama, I want to hear about how things are going for *you*. It always seems like we're talking about whatever drama *I* have and not so much about yours."

Beatrice chuckled. "Do I have drama? You forget I live with Wyatt. He's the one who helps dissolve drama."

"Well, I'm sure you have something going on. It wouldn't have anything to do with Flossie and Gail, though, would it?"

Piper now looked a little concerned. She was never one to get in the way of anything Beatrice took on, although she did worry about her when she got entangled in local murders. Which seemed to happen more often than not.

"It might have to do with them a little. I've somehow become a person that other people like to talk with to sort things out," said Beatrice slowly.

"I can completely believe that. After all, that's what I've been doing! So you've been hearing information about the case?"

"Well, maybe. Some of it could fall under the heading of local gossip, but some of it might actually be pertinent. The important thing is that I've been filling Ramsay in or having the people I'm talking to fill him in. It can't hurt."

"Anything that helps get Dappled Hills back to normal," said Piper. "That's all anyone's been talking about lately. Do you think Ramsay is close to an arrest?"

"That I don't know. But you're right—it's all anyone is talking about. I think he has plenty of leads to investigate."

Piper, in an effort to get their visit off the topic of murder, asked her how things were going at church and Beatrice filled her in. When they heard some happy nonsensical singing coming through the monitor, they grinned and Piper collected Will and his things and left for home.

The next morning after a lovely breakfast of fruit, granola, and yogurt with Wyatt, Beatrice decided it was time to run the rest of the errands she'd been putting off. There was a library book to return (she'd finished her book the night before during a quiet evening with Wyatt) and one to pick up. There were prescriptions that had been languishing at the pharmacy for her to collect. And she needed one more ingredient if she was ever going to cook the shrimp and rice she'd been planning on making.

At the library, she waved to Alice at the circulation desk and then headed over to the shelves where the librarians placed the books on hold. There she spotted Trina Wallace, thumbing through a quilting book.

"Well, hi there," said Trina with a smile. "Good to see you, Beatrice."

"Looks like you've found some good reading," said Beatrice cordially, nodding at the book.

"This? I hope so. It's one of the ones Jessica recommended at her workshop."

"Are you going to give contemporary quilting a try?" asked Beatrice.

"I might. Or I might just try and understand the different techniques better. If I'm going to be a fair judge, I should know all the different methods, inside and out."

Beatrice said, "That's an excellent way of looking at it." And not, from what she understood, what Flossie had done. Maybe Trina was trying to use Flossie as an example of what *not* to do. "I'm so glad that you're still pursuing judging."

"Me too. It was a setback, for sure, but there's no reason why a bad recommendation letter should totally derail me from applying again. Anyway, I'm glad to see you, Beatrice. I was wondering if you'd heard about a service for Gail. I figured Wyatt would probably be the one planning it."

Beatrice said, "He's been speaking with Marion about it and I gather they're planning on a service in a couple of days. I believe it should be listed online on the funeral home's site."

"Thanks." Trina blinked, clearing tears from her eyes. "I just can't believe she's gone. She was one of my favorite people in the guild. I was really pulling for Gail and Ralph to end up back together again because they'd always seemed so good together. And at that point in a marriage, do you really want to throw it all away? When you're going into your golden years, that's when you most need the support of somebody else. I think they'd have found their way back to each other, but they simply ran out of time."

Beatrice nodded. "I felt like they were going to make it work, too. It's all just very sad. And frustrating, because it didn't have to be that way."

"I believe the affair was a real anomaly for Ralph, don't you? I can't picture Ralph as being serially unfaithful to Gail. I tend to blame Flossie for the whole thing. She was attaching herself to a vulnerable man." Trina looked stern, thinking about it. "It doesn't excuse what Ralph did, of course. But Flossie was a force to be reckoned with. She usually got whatever she wanted."

There was a note of bitterness in Trina's voice now. Perhaps she was reflecting on the fact that she wasn't able to always get what *she* wanted.

Trina continued, "Ralph must be feeling so incredibly guilty now about everything. I could tell he was so regretful about the affair and hurting Gail. He *looked* so different—like he was a shadow of himself. All he wanted was to get back together with her. Surely he's not responsible for Gail's death. I was out running errands when Gail died and I keep thinking it's such a pity I didn't have an errand that took me in the direction of Marion's house. Maybe I could have seen something that would make it clear that Ralph didn't do it." She shook her head. "I really need to run by Marion's house now and bring her some food. I'm sure she's really hurting."

"I had an interesting conversation with Marion just recently," said Beatrice with a nod.

"Interesting?" Trina asked.

"Yes. Oh, she really appreciated everyone's support before Gail died and I'm sure it's much the same now that she's gone. She mentioned your coming by, too, Trina. She's holding up fairly well, under the circumstances. But I'm sure she'll really appreciate the company right now."

"I'm sure she would," said Trina somberly. "How terrible it must have been for her to check on her daughter and find her dead like that. It's the last thing she would have been expecting. Gail was a lovely person."

The unspoken words were that Flossie wasn't so lovely. Beatrice asked slowly, "Have you had any more thoughts about what must have happened with Flossie? I know it's a terrible topic, but I just can't seem to stop myself from mulling it all over. It was what kicked all of this off."

Trina pressed her lips together and then said, "It must have been Alice. I do really hate saying that, but it makes the most sense. Those two sisters had a really challenging relationship, which was basically entirely Flossie's fault. I bet Alice must have been completely horrified when Flossie abruptly decided to move to town."

"I believe you're right. Flossie really upset the applecart sometimes and Alice is always so careful not to make waves."

Trina said briskly, "I don't think Alice *planned* to do it, mind you. I'm sure she must have just lashed out at Flossie in total frustration, without even thinking. She probably went over there to fuss at Flossie for sending a nasty recommendation or for being discouraging to Jessica. Then she just got overwhelmed with anger at her. Flossie could be awfully smug, couldn't she, and there she was making a gourmet meal and not caring at all about Jessica or me or anyone else she hurt. Then Alice must have had to eliminate Gail because she suspected her or actually knew something. Maybe Gail was driving over to speak to Flossie and saw Alice's car there. We just don't know. Anyway! Enough of all this. I for one don't plan on having Flossie's duplicity hold me back, as I mentioned before. I'll judge some regional shows, network, and reapply. And I'll find some folks to give me a *real* recommendation."

Beatrice was frowning, trying to latch onto a thought she had—something spurred by what Trina had said. But it slipped away like quicksilver. She said in a distracted tone, "There are certainly plenty of people who can give you a reference. You'll make the perfect judge—you're organized, fair, and you're clearly continuing your education on quilting." Beatrice gestured to the book Trina held. "I'm sure they'll accept you. One person's opinion shouldn't stand for that much."

Trina nodded, looking a little distracted, herself. "Things will work out...they always do. And, from what I hear, Jessica is moving forward, too. Tell me how things are going with you. How is Wyatt doing?"

"Oh, he's doing well. He's keeping really busy, though. He has lots of meetings at the church this afternoon and even into next week. And, of course, he has Gail's funeral to plan."

Trina nodded solemnly. "He'll do a marvelous job, as always."

"Yes." Beatrice smiled at Trina. "Well, I should be heading out. I have a few more errands to run today. Hope you enjoy your quilting book."

Trina gave her a tight smile in return, seemingly never able to completely unwind. "Thanks. I plan on it."

Chapter Sixteen

AS BEATRICE WAS COMING out of the library, she saw Meadow pushing Will in a stroller on the way in. She smiled. She should have known that Meadow was going to be dying for the opportunity to see the baby after being thwarted the day before. Then she saw a figure spryly hurrying along behind them.

"Beatrice!" beamed Meadow. "Look, Will, here's your Nana. What a nice surprise. Picking up some indecipherable fiction, I suppose?" She peered at Beatrice's book.

"Just something Ramsay recommended to me."

Meadow chuckled. "Then indecipherable is likely an understatement."

"Usually, that's the case, but this one is supposed to be pure fun." She held up the novel, *The Thursday Murder Club* for Meadow's doubtful perusal. Then she added, "Did you realize you're being tailed?"

Meadow's eyes grew big and she quickly glanced behind her. "Oh no. I don't think I want to deal with Miss Sissy again today. Chasing her down for her dental appointment was bad enough."

But Miss Sissy called out to her and Will, hearing the old woman, crowed out a greeting. Meadow sighed. "Too late. Oh well."

Miss Sissy sprang up the steps of the library and gave Will a quick cuddle before glaring suspiciously at Meadow.

"No dental appointments today, Miss Sissy," said Meadow in a reassuring voice. "We're just going to pick up a couple of board books for Will to read and then we were going to head over to the Patchwork Cottage to see Maisie."

Will adored Maisie the shop cat. It seemed to be mutual as Maisie was a most unusual cat. Ordinarily, cats weren't too fond of the unexpected movements of babies.

Beatrice followed them back into the library because she rarely missed an opportunity to visit with her grandson. Will carefully considered a bunch of colorful and enticing cardboard books before deciding on several that had cats and dogs featured prominently on the cover. They checked out the books and then headed back out to walk to the quilting shop.

The bell rang as they walked in and Posy came over to greet them. It was actually quiet in the shop and looked like the perfect time to catch up. They all settled in the seating area in the middle of the store . . . after Miss Sissy had taken several of Posy's brownies from the snack area.

Tiggy, Savannah and Georgia's aunt was there, too and walked over, beaming at them. "Well, hello there!" she said cheerfully in her robust way. "What a nice surprise to see you all."

Will showed off his baby teeth in a wide grin and Tiggy swooped down to give him a kiss on the top of his head. "The cutest baby in the world," she proclaimed in a reverent voice.

Will grinned again as if he'd understood every word.

Tiggy sat next to Beatrice on the sofa and Beatrice asked, "How is everything going?"

Meadow snorted. "Beatrice is being delicate. We all really want to know how *Dan* is!"

Tiggy laughed and turned a light shade of pink. Dan was one of the main reasons Tiggy had decided to move to Dappled Hills permanently—she had started out in town just to visit with Savannah and Georgia. But she and Dan had embarked on a relationship and had been dating for some months.

"Dan is doing great," she said in a rush. "Beatrice, did Wyatt tell you that Dan has a new project at the church?"

"No, I didn't know that. But he's the perfect candidate to do anything over there." He was. Dan seemed to be able to do everything and actually showed up for work on time, unlike so many contractors Beatrice had dealt with in the past. He was a hardworking guy.

"He's painting the Sunday School classrooms. They're the most cheerful colors now," said Tiggy with enthusiasm. "And he's even painted some simple murals—rainbows and an ark and things—on the walls of the younger children's rooms."

"I can't wait to see them," said Beatrice. "Before I forget, how are you enjoying your new place?"

"Oh, it's wonderful. I like the duplex so much more than the apartment I had before. The apartment was fine, I guess, but the upstairs neighbors seemed like they stomped around all day and all night. Honestly, they sounded like elephants. My neighbor in the other half of the duplex is an elderly lady who is as quiet as a mouse and very sweet. I try to give her a hand when she goes to the grocery store and help bring her groceries in. And I get my own little yard! The duplex takes care of mowing the lawn and trimming the bushes, of course, but they don't mind if I plant flowers or put up birdfeeders or things like that. Posy has gotten me set up with some of the most charming feeders and birdhouses that she made!"

Posy quickly said, "Cork actually made them—all I did was decorate them."

"Well, you both did an amazing job," said Tiggy. "I feel like I've really settled in to Dappled Hills now. Like I'm home. I only wish I'd moved here years ago."

Tiggy and Posy chatted for a few minutes about the types of birds Tiggy had seen and whether putting out safflower seed might keep the birds happy while discouraging the squirrels that were trying to take over the feeder.

Beatrice watched as Will was fascinated by the bow Maisie the shop cat was wearing and reached out to gently touch the fabric, which was displaying Winnie the Pooh characters. The cat curled up happily in a sunbeam on the floor next to Will and wasn't bothered at all by his curiosity.

The bell on the shop's door rang again and June Bug scurried in with Piper next to her. They gave a cheerful wave to the group and joined them.

"I met up with June Bug on her way over," said Piper. "She helped me track down Meadow and Will."

Meadow's eyes were wide. "Was I un-trackable for a while?"

Piper said with a smile, "Maybe your phone volume is turned down."

Meadow frowned and rifled through her large purse. "Mercy! I must have forgotten to put my phone in my bag. I was so intent on trying to pack up Will's bag that I completely neglected my own."

Beatrice thought that Piper was really very understanding. Most mothers wouldn't have been pleased about having to track down their baby all through Dappled Hills.

Posy asked, "How are things going with your quilt, June Bug?"

The little woman gave a shy smile. "It's coming along. Thought I might try that rotary cutter you mentioned."

"Oh, the ergonomically-designed one?"

June Bug nodded.

Meadow said, "Gosh, yes. Those cutters help me out so much. My old hands just can't handle the regular rotary cutters anymore."

"June Bug is working on a garden quilt pattern," said Posy with a smile.

Everyone murmured. Beatrice said, "Will you bring it to the next guild meeting? I'd love to see it." It was a complicated pattern that made for a gorgeous quilt.

June Bug shyly nodded again and Posy added, "It's going to be absolutely lovely. She's creating a gazebo with climbing flowers. And a few whimsical touches."

"I can't wait to see it," said Meadow fervently. "Maybe it will tempt me to try something a little more complicated, myself.

I've been doing easy-peasy things lately, just to keep my hand in it."

Piper said, "Well, you have been busy lately. I can understand it."

They looked over to where Will was still gently patting Maisie, who looked very pleased with herself.

Meadow said sadly, "I'm guessing you're ready to take Will back home?"

Piper said, "I thought I might take him on a stroller ride for a while. Maybe go through downtown and then around the park. I could stand to stretch my legs a bit today. I know Will played on the playground with Mama recently, but he might enjoy doing that again today."

Miss Sissy growled, "I'll come." It didn't seem to be a question or an offer, just a statement of fact.

Meadow quickly added, "I'll come too, that way I can be your official photographer along the way. I've gotten quite good at taking pictures with my phone, you know."

Beatrice thought that was a matter of opinion. Although perhaps there were fewer pictures featuring Meadow's thumb.

Piper said, "The more the merrier! Mama, are you coming, too?"

Beatrice saw that Meadow and Miss Sissy were already squabbling over who was going to put Will back in his stroller. She decided that having a quiet afternoon might be in order. "Oh, I'll let y'all enjoy the park. I have to pick up a prescription at the pharmacy and then run by the store. I'd better head on out."

Piper said, "Oh, it looks like Will is still wrapped up with Maisie. Is it okay if we give him ten more minutes with her?"

Miss Sissy and Meadow were agreeable to this, so they stayed behind and chatted more with Posy and June Bug as Beatrice left.

Later, she wished she'd recalled an uneasy feeling indicating that someone was following her. But she just didn't. She'd like to think that she was one of those intuitive people who could tell when something terrible was about to happen, but apparently, she wasn't.

She'd just picked up her prescription at the pharmacy and was walking out when she heard someone calling her name. It was Ralph.

Beatrice could tell by looking at him that he was not doing well at all. It looked like he hadn't washed his hair in days and his clothes were rumpled as if he'd slept in them. But it was his eyes that told most of the story. They were red-rimmed and bloodshot and absolutely exhausted.

"Hi Ralph," she said slowly. It seemed pointless to ask him how he was. "Everything must have been so hard these last days."

He gave a short laugh. "You just don't even know. All of the feelings are hard. There's nothing about this process that's easy. I'm having a tough time even getting in touch with Marion about Gail's funeral service. She was my wife!"

Ralph's voice was anguished.

"You haven't been able to reach Gail's mom?" asked Beatrice.

He gave a short laugh. "It's more like Marion isn't returning my phone calls. My *many* phone calls. Look, I know I screwed up, but I don't deserve to be kept out of planning Gail's service. I was wondering if you could pass on a message to Wyatt, since I've run into you here? I'd love to have Gail's favorite hymn as part of the service. I'm not sure Marion even knows it. It's 'Sweet Hour of Prayer.'"

Beatrice took out the small notebook that she kept in her purse and carefully made a note. "I'll be sure to let Wyatt know." And she was sure Wyatt would wince at the thought of having to ask Marion about adding the hymn to the service. With any luck, Marion would recognize that it *was* a good addition. She felt bad that Wyatt had to be in the middle of a family situation, although it sometimes seemed to come with the territory.

Ralph said in a low voice, "It's been so hard for me, Beatrice. I wonder if I'm cracking up—I feel like Gail's presence is around me all the time. Almost as if she's trying to tell me something. Or else it's just my guilt talking."

"Guilt?" asked Beatrice, managing a lighter tone than she was actually thinking she could.

"That's right. Oh, I had nothing to do with Gail's death, of course. Not directly, anyway. But I think what I did indirectly contributed to Gail dying. It's making me absolutely sick with worry."

Beatrice said slowly, "Ralph, both Wyatt and I would be happy to talk with you about this. You might also want to check in with your doctor though—it could be very helpful."

He shook his head impatiently. "It actually helps talking to you about it, Beatrice. I'm working everything out in my mind. It's all I can really think about. I need to tell somebody what really happened."

"Ramsay?" asked Beatrice hopefully.

Ralph shook his head again. "Maybe later. But I'd like to sort it all out with you first."

Beatrice nodded. "All right, Ralph." At least she was in a public place. She wasn't entirely sure what Ralph was going to say next.

Ralph took a deep breath. "When Flossie died, things didn't happen exactly as I said they did. And they didn't happen exactly as Gail said they did, either. You see, Gail was trying to protect me."

Beatrice nodded again. This was pretty much an established fact because Gail was worried about Ralph.

Ralph looked at her with a somber expression. "No, it's even worse than what you're thinking. She wasn't just protecting me because I was her husband and she felt a responsibility to me. She was protecting me because she'd *seen me* over at Flossie's house the evening Flossie died. Gail believed I'd killed Flossie and she was trying to cover it up by lying for me."

Beatrice felt her mouth go dry. "But you didn't murder Flossie?"

"No. Believe me, I had moments where I wanted to," said Ralph with a humorless laugh. "But I never laid a hand on her. I did show up, though, to speak to Flossie—I wasn't going to have dinner with her, no matter what she thought. When I got there, her door was slightly ajar. I knocked but there was no answer. I didn't want to stand outside Flossie's house for long because the town would be abuzz with gossip; I just walked in. That's when I found her. I knew I was going to be a suspect because of my affair with Flossie, but I figured it would be much worse if I was discovered with her body. I should have just called the police right then and told them what happened. Instead, I dialed 911 from her phone, hung up without saying anything, and wiped the receiver clean and left as soon as I could."

"But Gail saw you there."

"Exactly. She'd gone over to have it out with Flossie over the affair. Flossie had taken Gail by surprise when Flossie told Gail about the affair and Gail had just sort of crumpled up with the shock of it all. But Flossie apparently wanted to go over and really give Gail a piece of her mind. She saw my car over there and left. She said later that she didn't want the humiliation of interrupting me with Flossie . . . so she didn't see me leave." He shook his head. "She assumed later that I had murdered Flossie."

"Did you try to explain to Gail what happened?"

"I never got the chance." If possible, Ralph looked even paler than he had before. "Gail told me 'I *saw* you there.' I tried to tell her that I was there to break up with Flossie and not to kill her, but she wouldn't listen to me. In fact, she interrupted me every time. And then, she wouldn't even see me or take my calls. You know, of course, that she moved in with Marion. She wanted time to think."

Beatrice asked, "Why do you think this indirectly led to Gail's death?"

"I think she was so worried about what she'd seen that she was talking about it a lot with her friends. She might have admitted that she was there on the scene right after Flossie died. Maybe the murderer thought she might know something and felt they needed to get rid of her before Gail figured out who the real killer was."

Ralph's face was creased with anxiety and that terrible exhaustion. Beatrice said, "No matter what, Ralph, you know that you didn't cause Gail's death. Not directly nor indirectly. The person who killed her did that. They're the ones totally responsible."

The lines on his face eased momentarily and he nodded as if he wanted badly to believe it. He looked around them as if suddenly aware of their environment and the parking lot around them. "I'm sorry," he said abruptly. "I've been holding you up. You're running errands."

"Believe me, it's no bother at all. I'll pass along the message to Wyatt about the hymn at the service, but please make sure to call him yourself if you'd like to talk things over with him. He's a very good listener and really can give helpful advice."

Ralph nodded. "He is. And you are, too. Thanks, Beatrice."

A moment later, Beatrice was climbing into her car and giving Wyatt a quick call before she forgot. She got his voice mail and left a message. He must still be engulfed in the meetings he was scheduled for.

She drove home and sat on the floor for a few minutes to rub Noo-noo, who greeted her happily, her brown eyes dancing. "Let's go in the backyard, little girl," said Beatrice. She glanced around for her new library book. "For heaven's sake. Did I leave it somewhere?"

Beatrice thought about all her errands and groaned. It definitely hadn't been in the car, although she did check again just to make sure. Who knew where she might have left it? That would be her day tomorrow, obviously—to retrace her steps and see where the library book might have been left.

Instead of reading the new book, she headed to the hammock, thinking that watching the birds at the feeders and closing her eyes for a few minutes might be relaxing. And it was. The birds were chirping happily and there was a light breeze outside. She listened to all the sounds of the yard while taking some deep breaths.

She must have drifted off for a few minutes but she woke up abruptly to the sound of Noo-noo growling. Her eyes flew open and she saw Trina standing there. Trina, holding a fireplace poker.

Chapter Seventeen

"WHAT'S THIS ABOUT?" asked Beatrice, instantly alert. She struggled to sit up in the hammock. "What on earth are you doing, Trina?"

She was sharp because Trina's very stance was threatening. Her face was devoid of expression and she gripped the poker tightly. Noo-noo continued grumbling.

"I was following you, Beatrice," gritted Trina. "I knew after I talked to you that you knew something. It took me a little while, but I finally realized you'd figured it out."

Beatrice thought back over their conversation. Maybe she did know and hadn't had enough time to let it sink it. It finally did, however. "You knew Flossie was fixing a gourmet meal when she died," she said, slowly. "That's something that wasn't general knowledge."

Trina gave a short laugh. "Wasn't general knowledge, but apparently *you* knew all about it. Then I followed you, waiting for a time to get you alone. You had quite the busy afternoon."

Noo-noo gave a sharp bark and then a low growl. She didn't like the tone of Trina's voice.

"I saw you speaking in the pharmacy parking lot with Ralph. So Ralph knows, does he?"

Beatrice, feeling at an extreme disadvantage in the hammock, tried to sit up to swing her legs over the side.

Trina brandished the poker at her. "Stay where you are."

Noo-noo's barking became frantic and Trina shot the corgi a nervous look. "Tell your dog to be quiet."

"It's okay, Noo-noo," said Beatrice. But the good little girl didn't believe her.

"Ralph doesn't know anything," added Beatrice firmly.

"Sure he does. He was there at Flossie's house, you know. So was Gail. It was like a zoo at Flossie's when she died. Obviously, one or both of them saw me there or saw me leaving out the back. This town always has been too nosy for its own good."

Beatrice steadied her voice and said, "You killed Gail because you thought she'd seen you. But she'd seen *Ralph* there. She thought Ralph had killed Flossie, not you. You made a terrible error."

For a couple of seconds, Trina wavered. Then she blustered, "You don't know that. Gail told me she'd seen something when she was at Flossie's house."

"She *had*. She'd seen Ralph, like I just said. She was simply trying to confide in you about her worries that Ralph was involved in Flossie's death. But you drew your own, incorrect, conclusions and murdered her."

Trina made a wounded sound before gripping the poker and advancing toward Beatrice. "It doesn't matter," she said fiercely. "At this point, I just have to shut you up."

Noo-noo, beside herself, started making short lunges at Trina's legs, nipping her, and then backing off nimbly as Trina took ineffective swings at her with the poker.

"Noo-noo!" called Beatrice in alarm. But the corgi wouldn't stop. The last bite was less of a nip and more of a real bite and Trina cursed darkly.

Suddenly, at the gate into the backyard, stood a horrified Meadow, Piper, Will, and Miss Sissy taking in the scene. Miss Sissy gave a war-cry, grabbed a log from the woodpile, and launched herself at Trina.

Meadow, red in the face, bellowed, "What on *earth* is going on here, Trina?"

Piper, turning the stroller away so Will couldn't watch the scene unfold, looked on in horror. "Mama?"

Trina's eyes grew huge as Miss Sissy lurched at her, swinging the log back and forth without any coordination or sense of reserve at all. Trina dropped the poker, stepped rapidly backward, and put her hands up.

"Evillllll!!" hissed Miss Sissy.

Beatrice finally managed to get herself extricated from the hammock and scooped up Noo-noo, who was still frantically barking.

Meadow whipped out her cell phone, dropped it, and swooped down to pick it up again. She flamboyantly jabbed at the device until saying, "Ramsay? It's Meadow. Come arrest Trina in Beatrice's backyard *at once*."

Which is precisely what happened.

Chapter Eighteen

IT DIDN'T TAKE RAMSAY very long to arrive at the house and he came with sirens blaring and lights flashing. Meadow happily took Will back to her house so that Piper could look after Beatrice for a while.

Ramsay was reading a slumping Trina her rights and putting her in handcuffs while Miss Sissy glowered at everyone and disappeared inside Beatrice's house with Noo-noo, most likely to find something to eat.

Beatrice looked at Piper who was watching her with concern. "What gave you such excellent timing?" Her voice wasn't quite as strong as she would like it to be, but it was better than a few minutes ago when she hadn't been able to utter a peep.

"Your book did," said Piper, sitting them both down at the backyard table.

"My book?"

"The library book you accidentally left at the Patchwork Cottage." Piper lifted the novel out of the diaper bag she still carried and handed her the copy of *The Thursday Murder Club*.

"That's now officially my favorite book of all time," said Beatrice fervently.

Piper nodded, looking at Beatrice with worried eyes. "I'm going to step inside and call Wyatt to fill him in. He could probably hear the sirens and has got to be wondering what's going on. And I'll bring you a glass of wine to help steady your nerves a little."

It all sounded marvelous to Beatrice. Everything did. The sun looked brighter, the birds' singing was far more musical, the flowers were that much prettier. She was just absolutely delighted to still be in the land of the living.

The state police were there in minutes and took over from Ramsay, hauling a miserable-looking Trina off for questioning and processing. This freed Ramsay to come over and sit down at the wrought-iron table with Beatrice. Piper put the promised glass of wine in front of her and moved to go inside.

"No, it's okay—go ahead and take a seat," said Ramsay. Piper perched on a chair, looking as if she was still on high-alert.

"Wyatt on his way?" asked Ramsay.

"He'll probably be here any minute," said Piper.

Ramsay gave Beatrice a wry look. "Well, here we are again. You've gotten very good at wrapping up these cases for me."

"Apparently, I've gotten very good at putting myself in dangerous situations," said Beatrice with a dry laugh. "Luckily, I have friends to help me get out of them."

Ramsay took his notebook out and said, "Okay, do you think you can walk me through what happened?"

Beatrice took a sip of the wine. "That's going to mean taking a detour through Trina's twisted mind, but I think I can manage that. From what I understand, Trina picked up on some cues from a conversation we had. Cues that I didn't even realize I was sending out."

Ramsay nodded. "That was earlier today?"

"That's right." Beatrice thought for a moment. "Actually, I even made the mistake of telling her that Wyatt was wrapped up in meetings today."

That was the moment that Wyatt came rushing through the door into the backyard. Ramsay waved him over. Wyatt gave Beatrice a tight hug and then sat quietly, holding her hand at the table. Piper gave him a smile of greeting.

Ramsay said, "Beatrice was just telling me what happened so she can fill you in at the same time."

Wyatt gave her hand a squeeze and Beatrice took a deep breath. "Like I was saying, I inadvertently contributed to this problem by telling Trina that Wyatt was going to be at the church with meetings. I guess she figured she'd have a good window to . . . get rid of me. Anyway, during our conversation earlier at the library, Trina had made a flippant comment. Something like, 'only Flossie would end up dying while making a gourmet meal.' That kind of thing."

Ramsay raised his eyebrows. "Which was a dead giveaway."

Piper and Wyatt looked confused and Beatrice said, "The fact that Trina was cooking something fancy was something Ramsay was keeping quiet. And it *was* a dead giveaway, but I'd had a busy day and it didn't really sink in until later on. But it must have registered on some level and I suppose I frowned or was looking like I was trying to process her statement because Trina realized she'd messed up. She said she started following me around this afternoon."

"Where did you go?" asked Ramsay.

Beatrice chuckled. "I kept her busy. I spent a good deal of time at the Patchwork Cottage, so she must have staked it out for a long while. I had a pharmacy visit, too. And I ran by the store. Along the way, I ran into Ralph in a parking lot."

Ramsay's animated eyebrows rose again.

Wyatt squeezed her hand and said, "I did get your message about Ralph and the service."

Beatrice gave him a smile. "Good. Ralph is really a mess right now. I hope that having Trina apprehended for the murders will help give him a sense of resolution or closure. And maybe that will make Marion more open to letting him plan Gail's funeral service."

Ramsay said, "What did you and Ralph discuss? Out of curiosity."

Beatrice hesitated. "He spoke to me in confidence, but considering the circumstances, I'll fill you in because it ties into Trina's motives. Ralph apparently found Flossie's body. He'd gone over there to try and break their relationship off, realized she was dead, and quickly left, fearing he'd be blamed for it. Apparently, Gail saw him leaving and drew her own conclusions later."

Ramsay frowned. "Gail was there at Flossie's, too?"

"That's right—to tell Flossie off, Ralph said. And Trina was there, too, of course, trying to leave the scene after the murder."

Ramsay's face was grim. "A regular party over there. So Gail thought Ralph had done it. And Trina clearly thought that Ralph or Gail might have seen her leaving."

"Exactly. When she spotted me speaking with Ralph this afternoon, that must have helped corroborate that I knew something. She'd already killed twice and she was prepared to kill again to keep out of jail."

Wyatt squeezed Beatrice's hand and she squeezed it back.

"So Trina came over just a few minutes ago, believing that Wyatt wasn't here and she might have opportunity to get rid of Beatrice," said Ramsay.

Wyatt sighed. "Believed correctly. I was tied up at the church with everything from a staff meeting to a meeting with the elders on the church renovations. I wish I'd been here."

Piper said, "And I wish I'd been here earlier."

Beatrice nodded. "I'd fallen asleep in the hammock and by the time I woke up, couldn't extricate myself from it quickly enough. Trina just walked right into the backyard through the gate holding that fireplace poker."

"The poker was from her house, right?"

"Yes. Our front door was locked." Beatrice smiled at Wyatt. "Noo-noo was positively ferocious."

Wyatt chuckled, the lines on his face easing momentarily. "She didn't care for Trina, I'm guessing?"

"She did *not*. Noo-noo could tell immediately that Trina was up to no good."

Ramsay gave a wry smile. "We should deputize her. That kind of intuition is a skill we could use at the station."

"Besides nipping at Trina, she was also making a lot of racket. A *lot* of racket."

Piper said, "That's how we knew something was really wrong. I've never heard Noo-noo sound like that before. We went right around to the back yard instead of knocking at the front door."

Wyatt said fervently, "There will be lots of treats for Noo-noo tonight."

Ramsay said, "Well, that must have been quite a scene that they came up on. Meadow will likely never stop talking about it."

"Meadow was very indignant over it all. And Miss Sissy was just about as ferocious as Noo-noo," said Beatrice with a fond smile. "Trina dropped the poker right away."

Wyatt said, "What made everyone come over at exactly the perfect time?"

Beatrice gave a shaky smile. "This." She picked up the book from the table and showed to Wyatt and Ramsay.

Piper said, "We were returning the book to Mama."

"An excellent book," said Ramsay, looking at the cover of *The Thursday Murder Club*.

"It's the best book ever, in my way of thinking," said Beatrice. "I'd absentmindedly left it at the Patchwork Cottage and they were returning it to me after they visited the park and playground with Will."

Ramsay carefully closed his notebook. "Well, I have to say I'm glad this is over. It's always good to have Dappled Hills return to a sleepy little town. But I'm sorry you had to go through this, Beatrice. I hope you don't have any bad dreams tonight."

Wyatt said sadly, "That might be kind of hard to avoid."

Ramsay left to join the state police at the station and be in on the interview with Trina. Piper frowned and said, "Where did Miss Sissy go?"

Beatrice said dryly, "I think she's probably eating up the contents of our pantry."

"I'll go in and check on her," said Piper.

Beatrice stood up, giving Wyatt's hand a squeeze. "Actually, I think I'm ready to head inside, too. I'd been planning on cooking tonight, but leftovers are sounding pretty good right now."

"How about if we order some pizza?" asked Wyatt. "We haven't done that in ages and we really liked the Hawaiian pizza at the place downtown last time."

"That's the perfect idea. Pizza is great comfort food," said Piper.

"I thought you were wanting to eat some salads after all the good Southern cooking the ladies from the church have been making," said Beatrice, a twinkle in her eyes.

"Oh, that starts tomorrow," said Wyatt cheerfully. "Isn't that what people always say about diets? Piper, do you want to join us?"

"No thanks—I need to collect Will from Meadow's house and then figure out supper for Ash and me. Y'all enjoy the food . . . and the peace and quiet." Piper gave Beatrice a tight hug.

The pizza came in not long after Piper left. It was hot, the cheese was perfectly melted, and the toppings were fresh. Beatrice found herself eating a lot more than she realized she even had room in her stomach for.

After they ate, Wyatt asked, "Want to check out that new TV show we were talking about the other day?"

"It's not a crime show, is it?" asked Beatrice with a wry smile.

Wyatt chuckled. "Definitely not. I wouldn't foist one on you after your day today. It's a British comedy."

"Sounds right up my alley," said Beatrice. She wasn't ready to turn in yet, but she hoped the show wasn't too tough to follow. Between the busy, complicated day and the heaviness of the pizza, she was starting to feel sleepy.

They sat on the sofa together with Noo-noo lying halfway on Beatrice's lap. The show was nicely distracting and she and Wyatt laughed throughout.

After it was over, Beatrice's mind wandered back to the events of the day. Wyatt put his arm around her for a hug. "Are you okay?" he asked.

She nodded. "I am. I was just thinking about the different people involved in these deaths. I feel especially bad for Ralph. Now he's adjusting to life without Gail. And I wonder if Flossie's death might have hit him harder than he thought, too. After all, he must have cared for Flossie a little, no matter how angry she made him."

Wyatt said, "Now he's having to face living without either one of them. I did have a conversation with Ralph earlier today, though . . . he was one of the meetings I had scheduled. Without telling you the details of what we discussed, he did express a strong interest in throwing himself into work for the church."

"Oh, good. That sounds like a great way to keep himself busy and distracted while doing something meaningful at the same time. Is he doing more tech work for the church, then?"

Wyatt said, "There's some of that, yes. He also wanted to make a donation in Gail's name to set up a small computer lab for our Sunday school classes. We could use the computers to supplement the Bible lessons the kids learn and for our Vacation Bible School events."

"That's wonderful to hear," said Beatrice, giving Wyatt's hand a squeeze. She knew that creating a small lab was one task the church had been hoping to do for a while.

Wyatt squeezed her hand back. "He's not just focusing on technology this time, though—he's planning on branching into mission work. Habitat for Humanity, the homeless shelter in Lenoir, and the church's clothes closet."

"That makes me feel better about Ralph," said Beatrice. "He's been looking so distraught lately. I wasn't sure what was going to happen to him. But between the volunteer work and getting justice for Gail and Flossie, he should be feeling better soon."

"Who else were you worried about?"

"Mainly just Ralph. Alice had been a concern of mine earlier because she was so uncomfortable with Flossie's behavior that she sort of ducked out of sight for a while. But I've seen her out at the park lately when I was with Will and I think she's getting beyond that now."

Wyatt said, "Maybe it wouldn't hurt for me to call on her in the next couple of days and see how she's doing. I could encourage her to come to the concert the choir is putting on next week. I remember she enjoys music." He paused. "I do feel a little conflicted because part of me is sorry for Trina Wallace, despite the tragedies she's caused and the threat she posed to you."

Beatrice sighed. "I'd like to say that's just you being a generous person, but the truth is that I feel sorry for her, too. I don't think she planned on killing Flossie—I think it was a situation that just got out of control. But she surely did plan to kill Gail, and me, too, to protect herself. It's amazing how quickly it escalated from Trina simply wanting to be a circuit judge to covering up murder."

Beatrice's brow furrowed with concern as she thought about Trina's dramatically changed circumstances. Wyatt said gently, "You look completely exhausted. Do you want to try to go to sleep?"

Beatrice chuckled. "Sure. Although now Ramsay has me worried that I'm going to have nightmares all night. I'll give it a go, though."

But curled up that night with Wyatt and with Noo-noo sleeping at her feet, Beatrice didn't have any bad dreams at all.

About the Author

ELIZABETH WRITES THE Southern Quilting mysteries and Memphis Barbeque mysteries for Penguin Random House and the Myrtle Clover series for Midnight Ink and independently. She blogs at ElizabethSpannCraig.com/blog, named by Writer's Digest as one of the 101 Best Websites for Writers. Elizabeth makes her home in Matthews, North Carolina, with her husband. She's the mother of two.

Sign up for Elizabeth's free newsletter to stay updated on releases:

https://bit.ly/2xZUXqO

This and That

I LOVE HEARING FROM my readers. You can find me on Facebook as Elizabeth Spann Craig Author, on Twitter as elizabethscraig, on my website at elizabethspanncraig.com, and by email at elizabethspanncraig@gmail.com.

Thanks so much for reading my book...I appreciate it. If you enjoyed the story, would you please leave a short review on the site where you purchased it? Just a few words would be great. Not only do I feel encouraged reading them, but they also help other readers discover my books. Thank you!

Did you know my books are available in print and ebook formats? Most of the Myrtle Clover series is available in audio and some of the Southern Quilting mysteries are. Find the audiobooks here.

Please follow me on BookBub for my reading recommendations and release notifications.

I'd also like to thank some folks who helped me put this book together. Thanks to my cover designer, Karri Klawiter, for her awesome covers. Thanks to my editor, Judy Beatty for her help. Thanks to beta readers Amanda Arrieta, Rebecca Wahr, Cassie Kelley, and Dan Harris for all of their helpful suggestions and careful reading. Thanks to my ARC readers for helping to spread the word. Thanks, as always, to my family and readers.

Other Works by Elizabeth

MYRTLE CLOVER SERIES in Order (be sure to look for the Myrtle series in audio, ebook, and print):

Pretty is as Pretty Dies
Progressive Dinner Deadly
A Dyeing Shame
A Body in the Backyard
Death at a Drop-In
A Body at Book Club
Death Pays a Visit
A Body at Bunco
Murder on Opening Night
Cruising for Murder
Cooking is Murder
A Body in the Trunk
Cleaning is Murder
Edit to Death
Hushed Up
A Body in the Attic
Murder on the Ballot
Death of a Suitor

A Dash of Murder (2022)

Southern Quilting Mysteries in Order:

Quilt or Innocence

Knot What it Seams

Quilt Trip

Shear Trouble

Tying the Knot

Patch of Trouble

Fall to Pieces

Rest in Pieces

On Pins and Needles

Fit to be Tied

Embroidering the Truth

Knot a Clue

Quilt-Ridden (2021)

The Village Library Mysteries in Order (Debuting 2019):

Checked Out

Overdue

Borrowed Time

Hush-Hush

Where There's a Will (2021)

Memphis Barbeque Mysteries in Order (Written as Riley Adams):

Delicious and Suspicious

Finger Lickin' Dead

Hickory Smoked Homicide

Rubbed Out

And a standalone "cozy zombie" novel: Race to Refuge, written as Liz Craig